W9-CXY-360

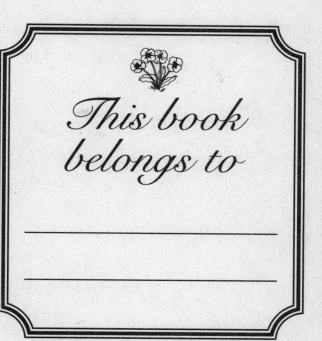

This book belongs to

_____

_____

Best Loved
SLEEPYTIME
TALES

Best Loved
SLEEPYTIME TALES

SIENA

THIS IS A SIENA BOOK

SIENA is an imprint of PARRAGON

Parragon
13 Whiteladies Road
Clifton
Bristol BS8 1PB

ISBN 0-75253-011-9

Printed in Great Britain

Designed by Mik Martin
Cover illustration by Terry Rogers

Contents

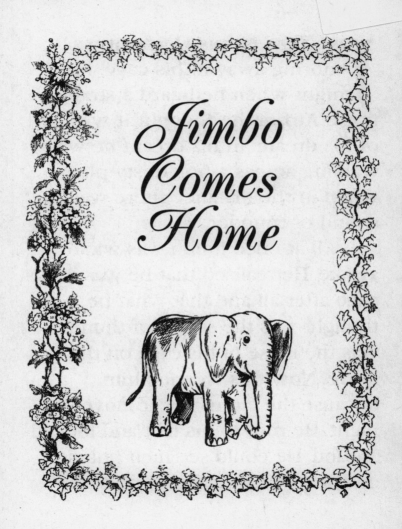

Jimbo Comes Home

JIMBO the circus elephant was snoring away in his cage one night when he heard a strange noise. At first he thought it was part of his dream. In his dream he was walking across a hot, dusty plain while in the distance there was the sound of thunder.

All at once Jimbo was wide awake. He realised that he was in his cage after all and that what he thought was the sound of thunder was the noise of his cage on the move. Now this worried him, because the circus never moved at night. He rose to his feet and looked around. He could see men pulling on the tow bar at the front of the

cage. These were strangers — it
certainly wasn't Carlos his trainer!
Jimbo started to bellow, "Help! Stop
thief!" But it was too late. His cage
was already rumbling out of the
circus ground and down the road.

Eventually, the cage passed
through a gate marked 'Zipper's

Circus' and Jimbo knew what had happened. He had been stolen by the Zipper family, his own circus family's greatest rivals! Jimbo was furious. How had the thieves got away with it? Surely someone at Ronaldo's Circus must have heard them stealing him? But Jimbo waited in vain to be rescued.

The next morning, the thieves opened up Jimbo's cage and tried to coax him out, but he stayed put. In the end, after much struggling, they managed to pull him out. Once he was out of his cage, he took the biggest drink of water he could from a bucket and soaked his new keeper! He refused to cooperate, kicked over his food, and when he appeared in the circus that night he made sure he got all the tricks wrong.

"Don't worry," said Mr Zipper to Jimbo's new trainer, "he'll just take a little while to settle down. Soon he'll forget that he was once part of Ronaldo's Circus." But Jimbo didn't forget for, as you know, an elephant never forgets.

The other animals in Zipper's Circus had all been stolen from other circuses, too. "You'll just have to get used to it here," said one of the chimps to Jimbo. "It's not so bad really." But Jimbo decided he was going to try and escape.

One night, a mouse passed by his cage. "Hello," called Jimbo mournfully, for by now he was feeling very lonely, and no-one had cleaned his cage out for days.

"Hello!" said the mouse. "You don't look very happy. What's the matter?" Jimbo explained how he had been stolen and wanted to escape back to his own circus.

The mouse listened and then said, "I'll try to help." So saying, he scampered off and soon he was back with a bunch of keys. Jimbo was astonished.

"Easy!" said the mouse. "The keeper was asleep, so I helped myself."

Jimbo took the keys in his trunk and unlocked the door to the cage. He was free! "Thank you!" he called to the mouse, who was already scurrying away.

Jimbo's first thought was to get back to his own circus as fast as possible. However, he wanted to teach those thieves a lesson. He could hear them snoring in their caravan. He tiptoed up, as quietly as an elephant can tiptoe, and slid into the horse's harness at the front. "Hey, what do you think you're doing?" neighed one of the horses, but Jimbo was already hauling the robbers' caravan out of the gate and down the road.

So gently did he pull the caravan
that the thieves never once woke
up. Eventually they reached
Ronaldo's Circus. Mr Ronaldo was
dumbstruck to see Jimbo pulling a
caravan just like a horse! Mr Ronaldo
walked over to the caravan and was

astonished to see the robbers still fast asleep. He raced to the telephone and called the police, and it wasn't until they heard the police siren that the robbers woke up. By then it was too late. As they emerged from the caravan scratching and shaking their heads they were arrested on the spot and taken off to jail.

"There are a few questions we would like to ask Mr Zipper regarding the theft of some other circus animals, too," said one of the police officers.

Mr Ronaldo, and Jimbo's keeper Carlos, were both delighted to see Jimbo back home again. And Jimbo was just as delighted to be back home. Then Mr Ronaldo and Carlos started whispering to each other and began walking away looking secretive. "We'll be back soon, we promise," they said to Jimbo. When they returned, they were pushing Jimbo's old cage. It had been freshly painted, there was clean, sweet-smelling straw inside, but best of all there was no lock on the door!

"Now you can come and go as you please," said Carlos.

And Jimbo trumpeted long and loud with his trunk held high, which Carlos knew was his way of saying, "THANK YOU!"

Maurice the Minnow's Dangerous Journey

Maurice the Minnow lived in a beautiful, reed-fringed pond in a clearing in the middle of a small woodland. He had been born one fine spring morning, and now he spent each day swimming happily in the shallows with all his little minnow brothers and sisters.

But life in the pond had its dangers, too! He had heard alarming stories about a kingfisher that would dive into the water from a branch overhanging the pond and grab tiny fish and swallow them down. And then there was the heron — a great, grey, stalking bird that suddenly loomed into the

shallows and snatched unsuspect-
ing fish with its great beak.

But the stories Maurice feared
most were the ones about Lucius
the pike. Lucius had lived in the
pond for longer than anyone could
remember. Woe betide you if you
met Lucius when he was hungry,
for he would dart out from his
hiding place among the water
weeds, and you would be gone!
Nothing ever escaped from his
huge jaws, which were lined with
needle-sharp teeth. Maurice had
heard tales of Lucius swallowing
fish bigger than Maurice could
imagine — not to mention ducks,
voles and other animals of the

pond. Why, there was even a rumour that Lucius had once snatched a dog from the bank and taken it down to the depths of the pond to devour it!

Maurice's mother had said that the best way to avoid meeting Lucius was to always stay in the shallows, and never swim across the pond, for it was in the deep, dark waters that Lucius loved to hunt.

One sunny summer's day, Maurice and his brothers and sisters were swimming in the shallows as usual, when suddenly he felt himself being lifted up and out of the water. The next thing he knew he was flapping helplessly in the bottom of a net, gasping for breath. Mercifully, he soon found himself back in the water again, but it seemed different now. It was light all around and there were no welcoming, sheltering weeds to hide in. And where were all his brothers and sisters? Next, to his horror, he saw a huge, unfamiliar creature staring at him. He'd heard no stories about anything as big as this! The creature's head seemed so close that Maurice felt certain he was about to be eaten. But just as suddenly the creature seemed to move away, and Maurice felt himself being carried along in this new, strange, watery world.

Maurice was wondering if he was to be trapped in this new, small pond forever when just as suddenly as he seemed to have entered the pond, he was now leaving it again. He felt himself falling down, down, until — with a splash — he was

back in his own pond again. Or at least, it seemed like his pond, but nothing was quite as familiar as it had been. Finding a clump of water weed, he immediately dived under it for safety, while he considered

"Hello, you're new here, aren't you?" a friendly voice said. Maurice looked round in surprise to find himself face to face with a frog. He told the frog about his horrible adventure while the frog listened patiently, nodding wisely from time to time.

"Well, we know what's happened to you, don't we?" said the frog when Maurice had finished. "You got caught in a little boy's fishing net. They're often about around here. I've no doubt the big creature you saw was just the little boy looking at you swimming in his jam jar full of water. And now he's decided to put you back. The only trouble is, you're far from home. You live on the other side of the pond. And to get you back means we have got to go on a very dangerous journey."

Maurice didn't like the sound of this at all, but he missed his family terribly and knew that he would never be able to get back home without the kind frog's help. So without more ado, the two of them set off for their journey across the deep, dark pond.

"Swim near the surface. It's safer," advised the frog, "but keep a close eye out for kingfishers."

They seemed to have been swimming for ages, when suddenly a great, dark shadow appeared beneath them.

"It's Lucius!" cried the frog in fright.

Before either of them could escape, they found themselves face to face with the dreaded pike.

"Well, well," leered Lucius. "I can't believe my luck! A frog *and* a minnow. Lunch and supper together if I'm not mistaken!"

So saying, he opened his enormous jaws and was about to swallow them whole when — BOINK! — a huge, flat stone landed right on Lucius's head. Dazed, Lucius sank slowly towards the bottom of the pond.

"Quick! It's our chance to escape!" yelled the frog. The two friends swam for their lives. Maurice kept thinking that any moment Lucius would reappear, but he needn't have worried. Lucius had too big a headache to think about hunting for a while yet!

Then suddenly Maurice was home. He recognised his own little part of the pond, and there

swimming in the shallows was his
family.

"I can't thank you enough," said
Maurice gratefully to the frog. "But
what *did* happen to Lucius?"

"You can thank the little boy
who caught you in the net for our

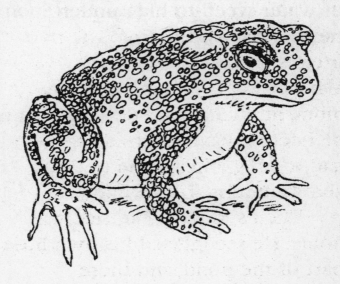

escape," said the frog. "He was skimming stones across the pond and luckily Lucius's head got in the way!"

Maurice decided that he'd had quite enough adventures for one day, and found himself a cosy piece of water weed to hide under. Soon he was fast asleep.

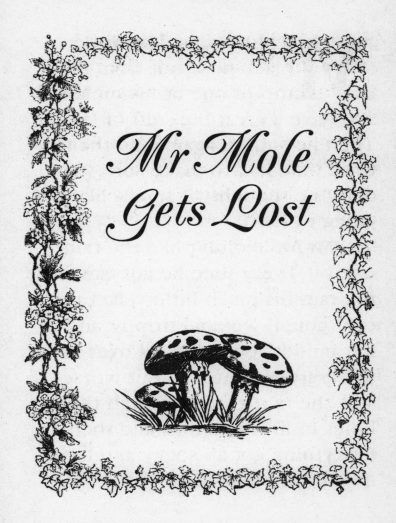

Mr Mole Gets Lost

MR MOLE poked his little black nose out from the top of one of his mole hills and gave a great big sniff of the air. Then he sniffed again. And then a third time just to make sure. "Oh dear," he thought, "it smells like it's going to rain."

Mr Mole didn't like the rain one bit. Every time he got caught in the rain his plush little velvet fur coat got all wet and drippy, and he left muddy footprints all over his underground burrow. But worse still, the rain got in through the holes in his mole hills and then everything got all soggy and took days to dry out.

Well, the skies got darker and darker, and very soon little spots of rain began to fall. Then the spots became bigger. And then bigger still. Before long, all you could see before your eyes were big, straight rods of rain bouncing off the leaves on the trees, pounding the ground and turning everything muddy and wet.

Mr Mole had never seen rain like it. He sat in his burrow in the middle of the meadow wishing it would stop. But it just kept raining and raining. Soon the rain started entering his burrow. First it went drip, drip, drip through the holes in his mole hills, and then it became a little river of water in the bottom of his burrow. Then the little river became a bigger, faster-flowing river and suddenly Mr Mole was being washed along by it. Through the tunnels of his burrow he went, this way and then that, as the water gushed and poured through his underground home.

The next thing he knew he was being washed out of his burrow completely as the rain water carried him off down the meadow. Down he went, not knowing which way up he was or where he was going. Now he was being washed through the woods at the bottom of the meadow, but still the water carried him on, bouncing and turning him until he was dizzy and gasping for breath.

Suddenly, he came to a halt. The rain water gurgled and trickled around him and then flowed onwards, as he found himself stuck firmly in the branches of a bush. "Oh dear," Mr Mole said as he got himself free. "Goodness me, where

can I be?" he thought. Mr Mole looked around him, but being a very short-sighted mole — as most moles are — he couldn't make out any of the places that were familiar to him. Worse still, he couldn't smell any smells that were familiar

to him. He was completely lost, far from home, and had no idea how to get back again. Now, to make things worse, it was starting to get dark.

"Woo-oo-oo-oo-oo!" said a voice suddenly. Mr Mole nearly jumped out of his moleskin with fright. "I wouldn't stay here if I were you," said the voice again. Mr Mole looked up and found himself face to face with an enormous owl. "Don't you know it's not safe in the woods at night?" asked the owl. "There are snakes and foxes and weasels and all sorts of nasty creatures that you really wouldn't like to meet."

"Oh dear!" was all Mr Mole could think of saying. He told the owl of his terrible watery journey and how he was lost and didn't know how to get back home again.

"You need to talk to Polly Pigeon," said the owl. "She is a homing pigeon and she lives near your meadow. She can show you the way home. But we'll have to find her first. Stay close to me, mind, and look out for those snakes, foxes and weasels I told you about."

Mr Mole didn't need telling twice. He stayed so close to the kindly owl that every time the owl stopped or turned round to talk to Mr Mole, Mr Mole bumped right into him!

Through the dark, dangerous woods they went. Every now and again, there would be an unfriendly noise, such as a deep growl or a hiss, coming from the dense,

tangled trees, but Mr Mole didn't want to think about that too much, so he just made sure that he never lost sight of the owl.

Finally, just when Mr Mole thought that he couldn't go a step further, they came to a halt by an old elm tree.

"Hallo-oooo," called the owl.

They were in luck. Polly Pigeon was waking up, and they found her just in time for she was about to continue her journey home.

"Please," said Mr Mole, "I'm afraid I'm terribly lost and don't know how to get back to my meadow. Will you take me there?"

"Of course I will," said Polly Pigeon. "We'd better let you rest here a while first, though. But we must go before it gets light."

So Mr Mole was soon trudging wearily back to his meadow, following as closely behind Polly Pigeon as he was able. Just as the first rays of sun lit the morning sky, Mr Mole smelled a very familiar smell. It was his meadow! He was almost home!

Soon, he was back in his own burrow. It was so wet and muddy, however, that the first thing he did was build some new tunnels higher up the meadow so that the rain wouldn't wash down into them so easily. Then he settled down to eat one of his supplies of worms, and fell into a deep, well-earned slumber.

Mr Squirrel Won't Sleep

IT WAS AUTUMN. The leaves were falling from the trees in the forest and there was a cold nip in the air. All the animals began to get ready for winter.

One night Mr Fox came back from hunting and said to his wife, "There's not much food about now it's getting colder. We'd better start storing what we can to help tide us over the winter."

"You're right, Mr Fox," replied his wife, as she gathered her cubs into their lair.

"I'd love to go fishing," said Mr Bear, "but I'll have to wait until spring now." He went into his den, shut the door tight and sealed it.

"Well, I'm off for a holiday in the sun," announced Mrs Cuckoo, preening her feathers. "See you all next year!" she called as she took to the wing and flew south.

Mrs Mouse ran by with a mouthful of straw. "Must dash," she squeaked, "or my winter bed will

never be finished in time." But soon she, too, was curled up with her tail wrapped around her for warmth.

Now only Mr Squirrel wasn't ready for winter. He danced about in his tree, leaping from branch to branch and chasing his tail. "Ha, ha!" he boasted. "I don't have to get ready for winter. I have a fine store of nuts hidden away, a beautiful bushy tail to keep me warm and besides, I don't feel in the least bit sleepy." And he carried on playing in his tree.

"Are you still awake?" snapped Mr Fox.

"Go to sleep!" growled Mr Bear.

"Please be quiet," squeaked Mrs

Mouse, drawing her tail more tightly about her ears.

But Mr Squirrel wouldn't go to sleep. Not a bit of it. He danced up and down all the more and shouted, "I'm having SUCH FUN!" at the top of his voice.

Winter came. The wind whistled in the trees' bare branches, the sky turned grey and it became bitterly cold.

Then it started to snow. At first Mr Squirrel had a grand time making snowballs — but there was no-one around to throw them at and he began to feel rather lonely. Soon he felt cold and hungry, too.

"No problem!" he said to

himself. "I'll have some nice nuts to eat. Now, where did I bury them?" He scampered down his tree to find that the ground was deep with snow. He ran this way and that trying to find his hiding places, but all the forest looked the same in the snow and soon he was hopelessly lost.

"Whatever shall I do?" he whimpered, for now he was shivering with cold and hunger and his beautiful, bushy tail was all wet and bedraggled.

All of a sudden he thought he heard a small voice. But where was it coming from? He looked all around but there was no sign of anyone. Then he realised that the voice was coming from under the snow. "Hurry up!" said the voice. "You can join me down here, but you'll have to dig a path to my door."

Mr Squirrel started digging frantically with his front paws and sure enough there was a path leading to a door under a tree stump. The door was slightly open — open enough for Mr Squirrel to squeeze his thin, tired body through.

Inside was a warm, cosy room with a roaring fire, and sitting by the fire was a tiny elf. "I heard you running around up there and thought you might be in need of a bit of shelter," said the elf. "Come and warm yourself by the fire." Mr Squirrel was only too pleased to accept and soon he was feeling warm and dry.

"This isn't my house, you know," said the elf. "I think it might be part of an old badgers' sett. I got lost in the forest and so when I

found this place, I decided to stay here until spring. Though how I'll ever find my way home, I don't know." A fat tear rolled down the elf's cheek.

"I have been a very foolish squirrel," said Mr Squirrel. "If you hadn't taken me in I surely would

have died. I am indebted to you and if you will let me stay here until spring, I will help you find your way home."

"Of course you can stay," replied the elf. "I'd be glad of the company." So Mr Squirrel settled down with his tail for a blanket and soon he was fast asleep.

Days and nights passed, until one day the elf popped his head out of the door and exclaimed, "The snow has melted, spring is coming. Wake up, Mr Squirrel." Mr Squirrel rubbed his eyes and looked out. It was true. There were patches of blue in the sky and he could hear a bird singing.

"Climb upon my back," Mr Squirrel said to the elf. "I'm going to show you the world." They set off through the forest until they came to the highest tree of all.

"Hold tight!" called Mr Squirrel as he climbed up through the branches until finally they reached the very top of the tree.

"You can look now," said Mr Squirrel, seeing that the elf had put his tiny hands over his eyes. The elf uncovered his eyes and stared and stared. He had never seen anything like it in his whole life. Stretching in all directions, as far as the eye could see, were mountains, lakes, rivers, forests and fields.

"What's that silvery-blue thing in the distance?" asked the elf.

"Why, that's the sea!" replied Mr Squirrel.

Suddenly the elf started to jump for joy.

"What is it?" said Mr Squirrel.

"I… I… can see my home," cried the elf, pointing down into the valley below the forest. "And there's my wife sitting in a chair in the sunshine. I must go home, Mr Squirrel. Thank you for showing me the world, for I should never have seen my home again without you." And with that he climbed down the tree and skipped all the way home.

Mr Squirrel made his way back to his own tree.

"Where have you been?" said Mr Fox.

"We've been looking for you," said Mr Bear.

"I'm glad you're home," said Mrs Mouse.

"So am I," said Mr Squirrel. "I've been very foolish, but I've learned my lesson. Now let's have a party — I've got rather a lot of nuts that need eating up!"

So the animals celebrated spring with a fine feast. And Mr Squirrel vowed not to be silly again next winter.

Mrs Mouse's Holiday

Mrs Mouse was very excited. All year she had been *so* busy. First there had been nuts and berries to gather in readiness for winter. Then she had needed to give her little house a big spring clean to make it nice and fresh. Now, as the warm sun shone down on the trees and flowers of her woodland home, she had promised herself a well-deserved holiday. But getting ready for holidays seemed to make one busier than ever! There was so much to do!

First she took out her little case, opened it and placed it carefully on her neatly made bed.

Then she rushed to her cupboard and selected some fine holiday dresses. Back to her case she scuttled and laid them in. Now she chose several pairs of shoes — a nice pair of sandals for walking along the front in, a pair of smart shoes for shopping in, an even smarter pair for going to dinner in, and another pair just in case!

"I'll need a couple of sun hats," she thought to herself, and so into the case they went as well. These

were followed by a coat, some gloves and a scarf (just in case the breeze got up and it became cold). Then, in case it became very sunny, in went some sunglasses, some sun cream and a sunshade. But, oh dear, there were so many things in the case that it refused to shut. She tried sitting on it, and bouncing on it, but still it stubbornly would not close.

So out from the case came all the things that she had just put in, and Mrs Mouse scurried to the cupboard again and chose an even bigger case. This time they all fitted perfectly, and she shut the case with a big sigh of relief.

Now she was ready to go to the seaside for her holiday. She sat on the train, with her case on the rack above her head, munching her hazel nut sandwiches and looking eagerly out of the window hoping to see the sea. Finally, as the train chuffed around a bend, there it was! A great, deep blue sea shimmering in the sun, with white gulls soaring over the cliffs and headlands.

"I'm really looking forward to a nice, quiet rest," she said to herself.

Her guest house was very comfortable, and so close to the sea that she could smell the clean, salty air whenever she opened her window. "This is the life," she thought. "Nice and peaceful."

After she had put her clothes away, she put on her little swimming costume and her sun hat and packed her beach bag. Now she was ready for some peaceful sunbathing!

At the beach, she found herself a quiet spot, closed her eyes and was soon fast asleep. But not for long! A family of voles had arrived on the beach, and they weren't trying to have a quiet time at all. The youngsters in the family yelled at the top of their voices, splashed water everywhere, and sent their beach ball tumbling all over Mrs

Mouse's neatly laid out beach towel.

Just as Mrs Mouse thought that it couldn't get any noisier, along came a crowd of ferrets. Now if you've ever sat on a beach next to a crowd of ferrets, you'll know what it's like. Their noisy shouting and singing made Mrs Mouse's head buzz.

Mrs Mouse couldn't stand it a moment longer. She was just wondering where she might find some peace and quiet when she spotted a rock just a little way out to sea.

"If I swim out to that rock," she thought, "I will surely have some peace and quiet there." So she gathered up her belongings and swam over to the rock. It was a bit lumpy, but at least it was quiet. Soon she was fast asleep again.

Just then the rock started to move slowly out to sea! It wasn't really a rock at all, you see, but a turtle which had been dozing near the surface. Off into the sunset it went, with Mrs Mouse dozing on its back, quite unaware of what was happening.

Eventually, the turtle came to a deserted island. At that moment, Mrs Mouse woke up. She looked at the empty beach, and without even knowing she had been sleeping on a turtle, she jumped off and swam to the shore, thinking it was the beach that she had just left.

Just then, the turtle swam off, and Mrs Mouse suddenly realised what had happened. For a moment she was horrified. But then she looked at the quiet, palm-fringed beach with no-one about but herself, and thought of the noisy beach she had just left.

"Well, perhaps this isn't such a

bad place to spend a quiet holiday after all," she thought.

And that's just what she did. Day after day she lazed on her own private beach with no-one to disturb her. There were plenty of coconuts and fruits to eat, and she wanted for nothing. She even made herself a cozy bed from palm leaves.

Eventually, though, she started to miss her own little house in the woods and decided it was time to get back home. First she took half a coconut and nibbled out the tasty inside. "That will make a fine boat to sit in," she said.

Next she found a palm leaf and

stuck it in the bottom of the shell. She took her little boat to the water's edge and, as the wind caught her palm leaf sail, off she floated back to the boarding house to get her belongings.

As she sailed back she thought, "This is the quietest holiday I've ever had. I may come back here next year!"

The Dog With No Voice

THERE ONCE LIVED a prince whose words were pure poetry. He amused the court with his witty, rhyming verse, yet his kind and thoughtful words made him popular with all. It was said he could even charm the birds from the trees.

One day, he was walking in the forest when he came upon an old lady with a huge bundle on her back. "Let me help," said the prince. He took the load and walked along beside the woman. They chatted away and before long they had reached the old lady's door.

Now the old lady — who was really a witch — had been listening intently to the prince's words. "What a fine voice he has!" she thought to herself. "I would like my own son to speak like that. Then maybe he could find himself a wealthy wife and we'd be rich for ever more!"

"You must be thirsty," she said to the prince. "Let me give you something to quench your thirst to repay you for your kindness." The prince gratefully accepted, and was

given a delicious drink which he drained to the last drop. He was about to thank the witch when he began to feel very peculiar. He found he was getting smaller and smaller. He looked down at his feet and saw two hairy paws. Then he turned round and saw to his horror that he had grown a shaggy tail! He tried to shout at the witch but all that came out of his mouth was a loud bark!

The witch hugged herself for joy. "My spell worked!" she cackled. "Come here my son!" she called.

There appeared at the door a rough-looking young man. "What's going on, my dearest mother?" he said in a voice that sounded familiar to the prince. Then he looked down and exclaimed, "Where did you find this poor little dog?"

Now the prince understood what had happened. "The old lady has turned me into a humble hound and given my voice to her son. Whatever am I to do?" he thought miserably. "I can't return to the palace. They'll never let a stray dog in." He turned with his tail between his legs and trotted off forlornly into the forest.

The witch and her son were delighted with his new voice. She made him scrub himself clean from top to toe and dressed him in the prince's clothes. "Now go," she said, "and don't return until you've found a rich girl to marry!"

The young man set off, eager to try out his new voice. Soon he was feeling very pleased with himself as he talked to passers-by. "What a very polite young man!" and "What a wonderful way with words," folk cried. "He could charm the birds out of the trees," other people said.

The witch's son travelled far and wide until at last he came to a castle where he spied a fair princess sitting on her balcony. He called to her and straight away she arose and looked down into the garden, enraptured by the sound of his beautiful voice. She was enchanted by his fine words and guessed they must belong to a prince. Soon the princess and the witch's son were chatting away merrily, and to his delight when he asked her to marry him she readily agreed. "For one with so beautiful a voice," she

thought to herself, "must indeed be a fine young man."

Meanwhile, the poor dog-prince wandered in the forest, surviving as best he could by foraging for roots and fruits in the undergrowth. Feeling truly miserable, he stopped to drink from a stream. As he dipped his long dog's tongue in the cool water, he caught sight of someone sitting on a bridge. It was a pixie, fishing with a tiny net.

"Cheer up!" said the little fellow, "I saw everything that happened and I think I know how we can get your voice back. Follow me!" And with that he was off, dancing away through the forest with the dog-prince trotting along behind. They seemed to go on forever, and the dog-prince was feeling very hot, and the pads of his paws were quite sore, by the time they reached the castle. He could see the witch's son in the garden calling to the princess on the balcony.

The dog-prince's eyes filled with tears, for she was quite the loveliest girl he had ever seen and he wished he could marry her himself.

"We will be marrièd today," the witch's son was saying in the prince's voice, "I will await you by the church, my fairest one." Seizing his fishing net, the pixie leaped high in the air. As the words 'my fairest one' floated up to the balcony, he caught them in the net and gave them back to the dog-prince.

As soon as he had swallowed the words, the dog-prince could speak again. "Thank you, little pixie," he cried, "but what can I do? Now I am a dog with a prince's voice. The princess will never marry me."

"If you want to break the witch's spell, you must go to the church — fast!" said the pixie. And with those words he disappeared.

Straight away, the dog-prince

ran to the church door. There was the princess looking most perplexed, for standing beside her was the witch's son — with not a word in his head. "I don't understand," she cried, "I thought I was to marry a silver-tongued young man, but now I find he is a dumb ragamuffin!"

"I can explain," exclaimed the dog-prince.

The princess spun around. "Who can explain?" she asked, for all she could see was a dog in front of her. "What a handsome dog!" she cried, bending down and kissing him on the nose. To her astonishment, the dog's hairy paws and shaggy tail immediately disappeared and there stood the prince. "But you're... but he..." she stammered looking from the prince to the witch's son.

Well, the prince explained everything that had happened, and after that he and the princess were married with great rejoicing. And as

for the witch's son? He wasn't a
bad young man, really, so the prince
taught him to speak again — with a
beautiful voice — and he married
the princess's younger sister.

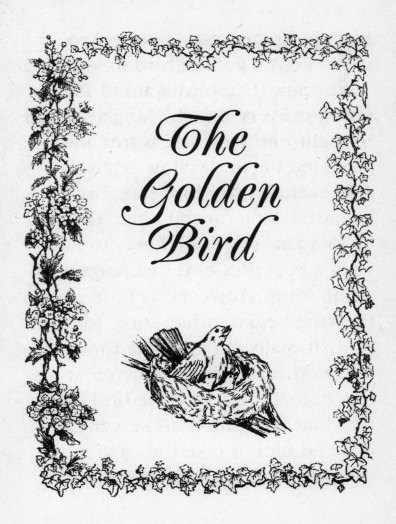

The Golden Bird

THERE WAS ONCE a king who kept a golden bird in a gilded cage. The bird wanted for nothing. Every day the king's servant brought him food and water and groomed his fine yellow feathers. And each day the bird sang his beautiful song for the king. "How lucky I am," cried the king, "to have such a beautiful bird that sings such a fine song." However, as time passed the king began to feel sorry for the bird. "It really isn't fair," he thought, "to keep such a handsome creature in a cage. I must give the bird its freedom." He called his servant and ordered him to take the cage into the jungle and release the bird.

The servant obeyed, and took the cage deep into the jungle where he came to a small clearing. He set the cage down, opened the door and out hopped the golden bird. "I hope you can look after yourself," the servant said as he walked away.

The golden bird looked about him. "This is strange!" he thought to himself. "Still, I suppose someone will come along to feed me soon." He settled down and waited.

After a while he heard a crashing sound in the trees, and then he saw a monkey swinging from branch to branch on his long arms.

"Hello there!" called the

monkey, hanging by his tail and casting the bird an upside down grin. "Who are you?"

"I am the golden bird," replied the golden bird haughtily.

"I can see you're new around here," said the monkey. "I'll show you the best places to feed in the tree tops."

"No thanks," replied the golden bird ungratefully. "What could an ape like you possibly teach me? You've got such a funny face. I expect you're envious of my beautiful beak," he added.

"Have it your own way," called the monkey as he swung off into the trees.

Some time later the golden bird heard a hissing noise in the undergrowth and a snake came slithering by.

"Well, hello," hissed the snake. "Who are you?"

"I am the golden bird," replied the golden bird proudly.

"Let me show you the jungle paths," said the snake.

"No thanks," replied the bird rudely. "What could a snake possibly teach me? With your horrid hissing voice, you must be jealous of my beautiful song," he said, forgetting that he had not opened his beak to sing yet.

"Very well," hissed the snake as

he slithered away into the under-growth.

By now the golden bird was beginning to wonder when his food would arrive. He began to imagine the tasty morsel that he hoped he would soon be eating. Just then he was aware of a movement on the tree trunk behind him. Looking up he caught a glimpse of a chameleon, lying camouflaged against the trunk.

"Good day," said the chameleon. "I've been here all the time, so I know who you are. You're the golden bird. I've heard you say it twice. It's a good idea to know where to hide in case of danger. Let me show you."

"No thanks," replied the golden bird. "What could an ugly brute like you possibly teach me? You must wish you had lovely feathers like me," he said, fluffing up his beautiful, golden plumage.

"Don't say I didn't warn you," muttered the chameleon as he darted away.

The golden bird had just settled down again when a great grey shadow passed over the jungle. He looked up to see an eagle swooping low over the trees. The monkey swung up to hide in the densest foliage near the top of the trees. The snake slid into the deepest part of the undergrowth.

The chameleon stayed quite still
but his skin colour became a
perfect match for the tree he was
on and he became totally invisible.

"Aha!" thought the golden bird.
"All I have to do is fly away and
that stupid eagle will never catch
up with me." He flapped his wings

and flapped and flapped, but he did not know that his wings had grown weak through living a life of luxury in the palace. Now the bird regretted his golden plumage and wished that he had dull brown feathers that would not show up in

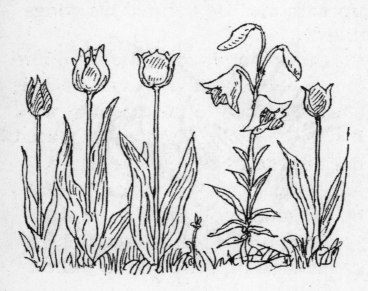

the forest clearing. For his fine yellow feathers made him easy to see. He was sure the eagle would come and gobble him up. "Help!" he trilled. "Please help me someone." Now he could see the eagle swooping down towards him with eyes blazing like fire and talons drawn.

At that moment the golden bird felt something close around his legs and pull him into the undergrowth. It was the snake. Then he was lifted up into the trees by a long, hairy arm and saw he was being carried by the monkey.

"Keep still," whispered the chameleon pushing him into the

centre of a large yellow flower. "The eagle won't see you there." And sure enough, the golden bird found that he was precisely the colour of the flower and the eagle flew straight past him.

"However can I repay you all?" exclaimed the bird. "You saved my life!"

"You can sing for us," replied the animals. And from then on, the monkey, the snake and the chameleon looked after the golden bird, and he sang his beautiful song for them every day.

The Greedy Hamster

THERE WAS ONCE a hamster named Harry. He was a very greedy hamster. As soon as his food was put in his cage he gobbled it all up, and then he would push his little nose through the bars in the hope that something else to eat might come within reach. From his cage he could see all manner of delicious food on the kitchen table — and the smells! The scent of freshly baked bread was enough to send him spinning round in his exercise wheel with frustration.

"It's not fair!" he grumbled to himself. "They're all eating themselves silly out there and here am I

simply starving to death!" (At this point he would usually remember the large meal he had just eaten and that his tummy was indeed still rather full.)

"If only I could get out of this beastly cage, I could feast on all the food I deserve," he announced to himself, and the thought of all those tasty morsels made his mouth water.

One night after the family had gone to bed, Harry was having one last spin in his wheel before retiring to his sawdust mattress. As he spun around, he heard an unfamiliar squeaky noise.

"That's funny," thought Harry.

"The little girl oiled my wheel only today. It surely can't need oiling again." He stopped running and got off the wheel, but the squeak continued. Harry sat quite still on his haunches and listened intently. Then he realised it was the door to his cage squeaking. The door! The door was flapping open. The little girl had not closed it properly before she went to bed. Harry did a little dance of glee. Then he went to the door and looked cautiously out in case there was any danger. But all seemed to be well. The cat was asleep on a chair. The dog was sleeping soundly on the floor.

Now, as well as being a greedy

hamster, Harry was also clever. Once outside the cage, the first thing he did was look at the catch to see how it worked. Yes! He was pretty sure he could work out how to open it from the inside now. Harry sniffed the air. There were some tasty titbits left over from a birthday party on the table. He could smell the sugar icing, and soon he was on the table,

cramming his mouth with odds and ends of cheese sandwiches and pieces of chocolate cake. When he had eaten his fill, he stuffed his cheek pouches with ginger biscuits and ran back into his cage, closing the door behind him.

"Good!" thought Harry. "Now I will never be hungry again."

The next night Harry let himself out of his cage and helped himself to food, and again the next night and the night after that. He feasted on everything and anything — nuts, bananas, pieces of bread, left-over jelly and slices of pizza were all pushed into his greedy mouth. Each time he returned to his cage he filled his cheeks with more and more food. He did not notice that he was getting fatter and fatter, although he was aware that he could no longer run round in his wheel without falling off! Then one night, he undid the door catch but found he was simply too wide to get through the door!

For a while Harry sat in a very bad temper in the corner of the cage. His cheeks were still bulging with food from his last midnight feast, but the greedy hamster wanted more. Then he had an idea. "I'll get that lazy cat to help," he thought. He squealed at the top of his voice until the cat, who had been dreaming of rats, woke up with a start.

"What do you want?" she hissed at Harry. Harry explained his problem.

"Of course, I'd be only too pleased to help," said the crafty cat, thinking to herself here was an extra dinner! With her strong claws she bent back the door frame of

the cage, until there was just enough room for Harry to squeeze through. Then, with a mighty swipe of her paw, she caught him and gobbled him whole. She felt extremely full, what with Harry and all his food inside her. She could barely crawl back to her chair and soon she was fast asleep again and snoring loudly with her mouth open. Inside her tummy Harry, too, felt very uncomfortable. Every time the cat snored, it sounded like a

thunderstorm raging around his head.

"I must get out of here," he thought, and headed for the cat's open jaws. But he was far too fat to get out again. Then he had another idea. Through the cat's jaws he could see the dog lying on the floor.

"Help! Help!" he squeaked. The dog woke up to a very strange sight. There was the cat lying on the chair snoring, but she also seemed to be squeaking, "Help!" The dog put his head on one side. He was very perplexed. Then he saw a pair of beady eyes and some fine whiskers inside the cat's mouth. It was Harry!

"Get me out of here, please," pleaded Harry.

Now the dog did not very much like the cat, so he was quite willing to help the hamster.

"I'll stick my tail in the cat's mouth. Then you hang on while I pull you out," said the dog. "But mind you don't make a sound and wake the cat, or she'll surely bite my tail!"

The dog gingerly put the tip of his tail inside the cat's open jaws, just far enough for Harry's little paws to grab hold. Then he pulled with all his might. Out popped Harry and out of Harry popped all the food he'd stored in his cheeks

— peanuts, an apple core and a slice of jam tart!

"Thank you, thank you," gasped Harry as he made a dash for his cage and slammed the door shut. "I think I'll stay in my cage from now on and just stick to the food I'm given!"

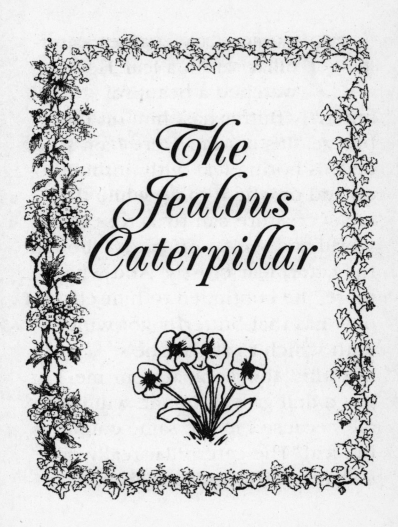

The Jealous Caterpillar

ONE SPRING DAY a green caterpillar sat on a leaf. He watched a beautiful butterfly flutter past him on the breeze. "It's not fair. Here I am stuck on this boring leaf with nothing to do and nowhere to go while that lucky creature can fly across the world and see far-off lands," thought the caterpillar crossly. "And what's more," he continued to himself, "not only has that butterfly got wings with which to fly, but he's beautiful, too. Look at poor me. I'm just a dull green. No-one will notice me because I'm the same colour as the leaf." The caterpillar really did feel very sorry for himself, and rather jealous. "Go and enjoy yourself. Don't worry about me," he called spitefully to the butterfly.

But the butterfly hadn't heard a single word the caterpillar had been muttering, and soon he flew away. The caterpillar suddenly decided that he was going to be like the butterfly. "I'll learn how to fly and I'll paint myself lovely colours so that I look beautiful, too," he thought. He looked around for something to paint himself with but, of course, there was nothing at all on the leaf. Then he tried to fly. He launched himself from his leaf and tried to flap his tail, but all he did was land on the leaf below.

Along came a ladybird. "Aha!" thought the caterpillar. "Here's a beautiful creature who knows how to fly. I'll ask her to teach me." So the caterpillar said, "Hello, I've been admiring your beautiful wingcase. Could you tell me how I, too, could be beautiful? And can you teach me to fly?"

The ladybird looked at the caterpillar. "Be patient and wait a while," she said wisely, "and soon enough you'll get what you want." And with that the ladybird went on her way.

"Whatever can she mean? She's just too proud to teach me," the caterpillar thought jealously.

Some time later a bee buzzed past and landed on a nearby leaf. "Aha!" thought the caterpillar. "Here's a beautiful creature who knows how to fly. I'll ask him to

teach me." So the caterpillar said, "Hello, I've been admiring your beautiful striped back. Could you tell me how I, too, could be beautiful? And can you teach me to fly?"

The bee looked at the caterpillar. "You'll find out soon enough,

young man," said the bee sternly. And with that he went on his way.

"Whatever can he mean? He's just too haughty to teach me," the caterpillar thought jealously.

Now a while later along came a bird. "Aha!" thought the caterpillar once more. "Here's a beautiful creature who knows how to fly. I'll ask him to teach me." So once again the caterpillar said, "Hello, I've been admiring your beautiful feathers. Could you tell me how I, too, could be beautiful? And can you teach me to fly?"

The bird looked at the caterpillar and thought to himself slyly that here was a very silly caterpillar, but he would make a tasty snack for his chicks. "Let's see if I can trick him," he thought.

"I can't give you wings and I can't make you beautiful. But I can show you the world. I expect you'd like to see the world, wouldn't you, little caterpillar?" said the bird.

"Oh, yes!" said the caterpillar in great excitement.

"Climb upon my back then, little caterpillar!" said the crafty bird.

The caterpillar did as he was told and the bird flew off towards his nest. At first the caterpillar clung tightly to the bird's back but soon he felt quite sleepy and eventually he dozed off and slipped from the bird's back. Down he fell through the air and landed on a leaf, but still he didn't wake up. Soon he was wrapped in a soft, brown, papery cocoon from which he would not wake up for a long while.

Meanwhile, the bird reached his nest. "Look at the treat I've brought you," he said to his chicks.

They looked very puzzled. "What treat, Dad?" one of them piped up.

"This nice juicy caterpillar," said the bird, shaking the feathers on his back. "Climb down, little caterpillar," he said. But of course there was nothing there. Now it was the father's turn to look puzzled, while the chicks laughed at him.
"Well, I must have dropped him," he said. "I've never done that before," he added. He flew out of the nest in search of the caterpillar but he was nowhere to be seen. Once he

saw a strange brown, papery parcel on a leaf, but in the end the bird had to return to the nest with his beak empty.

A long while later the caterpillar woke up. "I must get out of this stuffy wrapping," he thought, as he pushed his way out. He stood on the leaf and yawned and stretched. As he stretched, he noticed to his amazement two pairs of beautiful wings spreading out on either side of his body. "Are they really mine?" he wondered. He tried lifting and turning them and yes, he could make them work. He looked at his reflection in a raindrop and saw a lovely butterfly staring back at him.

"So the ladybird and the bee were right," he exclaimed. "How foolish I was to be a jealous caterpillar," he declared to a passing ant, "for now I am a beautiful butterfly after all."

The Lost Lion

ONCE THERE WAS a lion cub called Lenny. He was a very tiny lion cub, but he was sure that he was the bravest lion in all of Africa. When his mother taught her cubs how to stalk prey, Lenny would stalk his own mother and pounce on her. When she showed them how to wash themselves, Lenny licked his sister's face instead so that she growled at him. When the mother lioness led her cubs down to the watering hole to drink, he jumped into the water and created a huge splash that soaked everyone.

The other lionesses were not amused. "You'd better watch that son of yours," they said to Lenny's mother, "or he'll get into really big trouble."

One day the mother lioness led her cubs on their first big hunt. "Stay close to me," she said, "or you could get hurt."

She crawled off through the undergrowth with her cubs following on behind, one after the other. Lenny was at the back. The grass tickled his tummy and he wanted to laugh, but he was trying hard to be obedient. So he crawled along, making sure he kept the bobbing tail of the cub in front in sight. On and on they crawled until Lenny was beginning to feel quite weary.

"But a brave lion cub doesn't give up," he thought to himself. And on he plodded.

At last the grass gave way to a clearing. Lenny looked up, and to his dismay he saw that the tail he had been following was attached, not to one of his brothers or sisters, but to a baby elephant!

Somewhere along the trail he had started following the wrong tail and now he was hopelessly lost. He wanted to cry out for his mother but then he remembered that he was the bravest lion in all of Africa.

So what do you think he did? He went straight up to the mother elephant and growled his fiercest growl at her. "That'll frighten her!" thought Lenny. "She won't dare growl back!" And, of course, she didn't growl back. Instead she lifted her trunk and trumpeted so loudly at Lenny that he was blown off his feet and through the air and landed against the hard trunk of a tree.

Lenny got up and found that his knees were knocking. "Oh my," he thought, "that elephant has a very loud growl. But I'm still

definitely the bravest lion in all of Africa." He set off across the plain. It was getting hot in the midday sun and soon Lenny began to feel sleepy. "I think I'll just take a nap in that tree," he thought, and started climbing up into the branches.

To his surprise, he found that the tree was already occupied by a large leopard. "I'll show him who's boss," thought Lenny, baring his tiny claws. The leopard raised his head to look at Lenny, and then bared his own huge, razor-sharp claws. He took a swipe at Lenny with his paw. Without even touching Lenny, the wind from the leopard's great paw swept Lenny

out of the tree and he landed with
a bump on the ground.

Lenny got up and found that
his legs were trembling. "Oh my," he
thought, "that leopard had big
claws. But I'm still definitely the
bravest lion in Africa." He set off
again across the plain. After a while
he began to feel quite hungry. "I
wonder what I can find to eat," he
thought. Just then he saw a spotted
shape lying low in the grass. "That
looks like a tasty meal," thought
Lenny as he pounced on the
spotted shape.

But the spotted shape was a
cheetah! Quick as a flash, the
cheetah sprang away and as he did

so, his tail caught Lenny a blow that sent him spinning round and round in circles.

When Lenny stopped spinning, he got up and found that his whole body was shaking. "Oh my," he thought, "that cheetah is a fast runner." Then he added in rather a small voice, "But I'm still the bravest lion in Africa."

He set off again across the plain. By now it was getting dark and Lenny was wishing he was at home with his mother and brothers and sisters. "I wonder if they've noticed I've gone," he thought sadly as a tear rolled down his furry cheek. He felt cold and tired and hungry as he crawled into the undergrowth to sleep.

Some time later Lenny was woken by a noise that was louder than anything he'd ever heard before — louder even than the elephant's trumpeting. It filled the night air and made the leaves on the trees shake. The noise was getting louder and louder and the animal that was making it was getting nearer and nearer.

Lenny peeped out from his hiding place and saw a huge golden creature with big yellow eyes that shone in the dark like lamps. It had a great crown of shaggy golden fur all around its head and its red jaws were open wide revealing a set of very large white fangs. How it roared! Lenny was terrified and about to turn tail and run, when the animal stopped roaring and spoke to him. "Come here, Lenny," said the animal gently. "It's me, your father, and I'm going to take you home. Climb up on my back, little one."

So Lenny climbed up on his father's back and was carried all the way home. And when they got there his father told his mother and his brothers and sisters that Lenny had been a very brave lion after all.

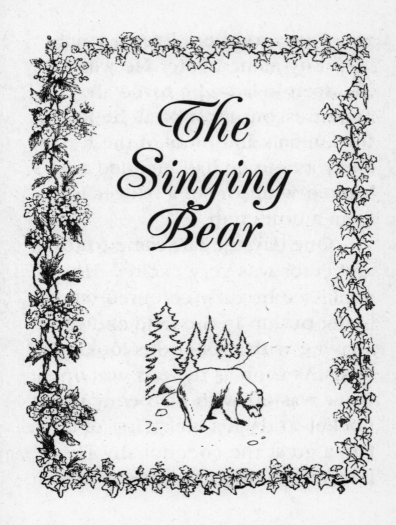

The Singing Bear

LONG AGO, there lived a young boy named Peter. He was a gentle lad who loved all creatures, but most of all he loved the animals and birds of the forest. Many a time he had mended a jay's broken wing, or set a badger free from a cruel trap.

One day, the fair came to town and Peter was very excited. He could see brightly coloured tents being put up in the field and carts arriving with mysterious looking loads. As soon as the fair was open Peter was off with his penny in his pocket to try his luck. First of all he had a go at the coconut shy. Then he tried to climb the greasy pole.

Finally, he used his last farthing on the tombola stall. He was about to head for home when out of the corner of his eye he caught a glimpse of a dreadful sight. Lying in a cage, looking sad and forlorn, was a large brown bear. On a small plate at the front of the cage was the bear's name: Lombard. He looked so dejected that Peter immediately vowed to set him free. The cage was strongly padlocked and Peter knew not how he could break the lock. He turned to make his way home, with the bear gazing pitifully after him.

That night, Peter tossed and turned in his bed. What was he to do? He wasn't strong enough to break into the bear's cage and his keeper would surely not agree to set him free. In the middle of the night, he resolved to return to the fairground to comfort the bear.

He slipped out of bed and made his way by the light of the moon back to the fairground. To his astonishment he found the bear singing a song to himself in a beautiful voice. For a while Peter listened to the lovely sound of the bear's singing. Then he had an idea. He remembered a piece of paper he had seen pinned to the palace gate.

"Don't cry, Lombard," he said. "I

think I know a way to get you out
of here. But first you must teach me
your song." The bear was happy to
oblige and soon the two of them
were singing the song together.
Then Peter said, "I must go, but I'll
be back tomorrow. And remember,
when you see me, be ready to sing
your song."

The next day, Peter put on his
very best clothes and set off for the
palace. Pinned to the gate was the
piece of paper, just as Peter had
remembered. On the paper was
written in a handsome script:
*The King Requires a Minstrel
with a Fine Voice. Apply Within.*
Peter knocked at the gate. He

was shown into a beautiful golden
gallery where a row of minstrels
were waiting to be auditioned. A
courtier rang a little bell for
silence, and in came the king. He
sat down at his great gold throne.

"Let the audition begin," cried the king. The first minstrel stepped forward. He sang a song in a sweet, high voice that tugged at the heart and reduced the court to tears. The next minstrel sang in a deep, rich voice that sent shivers down the spine, so that the birds in the trees stopped singing to listen. The next minstrel sang a song that was so witty and amusing that the entire court wept with laughter.

At last it was Peter's turn. He stepped forward, gave a deep bow and said, "I beg your majesty's permission to perform my song out of doors, so that all the wild creatures of the forest might hear it, too."

"What a strange request!" said the king. However, if the truth be told, he had grown quite sleepy listening to so many beautiful songs and thought the fresh air might liven him up. "Very well, but it had better be worth it!" he said, giving Peter a fierce look.

"Follow me!" called Peter. He led the king, the court and all the

minstrels out of the palace gates and down the road.

"Where are we going?" and "This is very untoward," they muttered.

At last they reached the fair-ground, but Peter didn't stop until he was in view of Lombard's cage. Lombard saw him and Peter winked at the bear.

"This is where I'd like to sing for you," said Peter to the king.

The king's royal eyebrows rose higher and higher as he looked around him. "Well, I must say this is very odd indeed! However, as we've come this far, we may as well hear your song. Proceed!" said the king.

Peter opened his mouth and mimed the words while Lombard sang. It was the most beautiful song that anyone had ever heard. By the end of the song, the king was sobbing tears of joy, mirth and sorrow all together.

"That was the finest song I ever heard," he said. "You have won the audition and I would like you to be my minstrel."

Peter took another low bow. "Sire," he said. "Would that I could accept, but in all honesty it was not I who sang but my friend, Lombard the bear."

Everyone gasped as they saw the bear in his cage.

For a moment the king looked furious. But then he began to smile and said, "I praise you for your honesty, Peter, and I would very much like to have Lombard for my minstrel. Chancellor, bring me the royal purse."

The king paid Lombard's keeper handsomely, who was then delighted to set the bear free. Lombard became the king's minstrel and was famous throughout the land, and from then on Peter went to the palace each day and sang duets with his friend, the bear. And it is said that, in the end, Peter married the king's daughter.

The Mouse's House

NOW THERE ARE those who enjoy keeping their things clean and tidy and there are those who don't. You can tell as soon as you step inside someone's front door which kind of home you are visiting. Of course, it is nice not to have to move piles of books and papers before you sit in a chair. And no one wants to find their plate covered in a thick layer of dust, but some people are *so* clean and tidy that it's no fun at all to pay them a visit. The Mouse was like that, as you will see.

The Mouse lived in a very cosy little tree-trunk house in the middle of Mendlesham Wood. She probably had been given a proper name when she was a baby, but everyone just called her "Mouse".

Mouse had always been proud of her home, and she had never been untidy. She liked everything to look just right, so that none of the other animals in Mendlesham wood could point their paws at her and say, "Have you *seen* the cobwebs in *her* house?"

But to begin with, Mouse was no more worried about dirt and dust than any moderately house-proud animal in the wood. The change was very gradual.

For a long time, she swept her front steps once a day. Then you might sometimes see her, especially in autumn, giving them a little extra sweep in the afternoon.

By the time of this story, she

was out on those steps half a dozen times a day.

"It's these horrible old leaves," she would say, if a friend protested that she was working too hard.

"But Mouse, you live in a *tree*!" the friend would say. "Of course there will be leaves."

"Not on my steps there won't!" replied Mouse stoutly, picking up her broom again.

Well, Mouse became as particular about the inside of her house as she was about her front steps. She was constantly dusting and sweeping and washing and wiping. She was a great plumper-up of cushions, too, and she had a hatred of spiders and their webs that would have been funny if it hadn't been rather worrying too.

"Out of my way," Mouse would say to a guest who had come to tea. "I saw one of those pesky little animals run under your chair. I can't rest until I've found him. The very thought of those eight muddy feet running over my floorboards makes me shiver and shake. Watch out! Don't spill your tea!"

It soon became something of a lottery to visit Mouse. You might have a perfectly lovely time, but on her worst days, Mouse was not a good hostess.

"Excuse me, but *did* you wipe

your feet as you came in?" she would ask, peering suspiciously at your shoes. "Perhaps you wouldn't mind doing it again."

Then, after you had dutifully wiped them up and down several times on the doormat, Mouse would make a big point of shaking the mat itself outside the door. Of course, that might mean that she felt the step needed sweeping as well. So you see what I mean, conversation at Mouse's tea parties was often a little strained.

Gradually, the animals in Mendlesham Wood became quite worried about Mouse.

"It isn't healthy to be so finicky,"

said the owl, whose own home was really none too clean. "Mouse is making herself ill worrying about things that don't matter at all. Why, when I visited her the other day, she told me I couldn't sit in the chairs because I'd flatten the cushions. I mean, what are chairs *for*? That's what I'd like to know."

"It was the same when I called to collect her grocery money," said the rabbit who lived under the old oak tree. "She wouldn't let me knock at the front door in case my paws were dirty. She was peering out of the window, waiting for me, so that she could catch me before I touched it!"

"That's dreadful," said the hedgehog. "Doesn't she know that a little bit of dirt is *good* for you. That's what I always tell my little ones."

Some of the others coughed and looked away. They knew very well that the hedgehog and her little ones were never invited to Mouse's house because it was well known by everyone that they had *fleas*. Mouse hated fleas almost as much as she hated spiders. Just because they hopped instead of scurrying, it didn't mean that their feet were clean. Very few tiny creatures were welcome in Mouse's home, although she did have a soft spot for moths, for some reason.

"Someone should talk to her," said the owl. "A close friend, I mean," he went on hurriedly, "not someone like me who is really only an acquaintance."

"The sad thing is that she really doesn't *have* any close friends any more," said the squirrel. "It is so uncomfortable to visit her now that nobody wants to do it. And it's hard to be close friends with an animal you hardly ever see. I can't remember the last time I visited Mouse's house, in fact. I miss having her as a friend."

"I think you're right," said the woodpecker. "I haven't seen her since I made that little attic window at the back for her a few years ago. She complained about the sawdust then, but she was nothing like so fussy as she is now. I don't think she could bear anyone to touch her house in any way."

The animals were well meaning, but they couldn't really

think of any way to help Mouse. In the end, it was a complete stranger who made a difference.

That winter was particularly cold. Even the trees shuddered as a howling, icy wind whistled around their roots and branches, frosting their twigs and chilling every little creature who lived nearby. All the animals huddled in their homes, doing the best they could to keep warm.

Mouse had a snugger home than most, especially as she always made sure that her window frames were free from draughts and her strong, tree-trunk walls were free from cracks.

But Mouse didn't like the way that frost made her windows look dirty, and snow had a habit of dropping from the branches above and falling with an alarming *plop!* on to her steps.

It was on a particularly cold and blustery night that Mouse had an unexpected visitor. She was sitting in front of her fire, sipping a cup of apple tea, when she heard a little squeal outside and then a hammering at her door. Mouse tried to ignore it at first, but then the dreadful thought occurred to her that someone might actually be damaging her home.

She pulled her shawl around

her shoulders and opened the door. Outside was a truly pitiful sight. A little mouse, no bigger than Mouse herself, was shivering on the doorstep.

"Please," he said, "could I come in to warm myself for a moment? I won't trouble you for long."

Mouse hesitated for just a second. She thought with horror of the mouse's wet little paws scampering across her sitting room. She shuddered at the thought of his cold, wet little body sitting on one of her chairs. She could imagine the way that he would shake his whiskers all over her carefully polished table. But Mouse could not bear to see another creature suffer, so she stood back from the door.

"Do come in," she said. "Er … the door mat is just here."

"Thank you so much," shivered the stranger mouse, as he stood in the middle of Mouse's sitting room. "I don't think I could have lasted much longer out there. It's no night for a mouse to be out."

"No, indeed," agreed Mouse. "Er … can I take your … er … coat?" She didn't really think that was the right word for the ragged, shapeless garment that the mouse held tightly around himself. But the mouse seemed to know what she meant and handed her the thin, wet cloth.

"I've been travelling for a long time," he said. "I'm on my way to see someone very special, but winter has been harder than I ever thought it would be. I should probably have put off my journey until the spring, but I was so eager to meet this person that I couldn't wait."

Mouse handed the stranger a towel to dry his whiskers before he shook them any more, but the visitor didn't seem to understand and wrapped the towel around his shoulders instead.

"Thank you again," he said. "I should introduce myself. My name is George."

The name sounded vaguely familiar to Mouse, but she couldn't think why.

"My name is Mouse," she said. "It sounds strange, I know, but I think it's what I've always been called. I can't remember when I was a baby."

George nodded and sat down

in the chair. Thankfully the towel was between him and the upholstery. Goodness knew when he had last taken a bath.

The newcomer was still shivering, so Mouse hurried to her neat little kitchen and made up a tray of hot soup, bread and juniper biscuits.

"I wasn't expecting visitors," she said, apologising for the makeshift supper. And all of a sudden she wondered why that was. There had been a time when her friends visited her every day, but she couldn't remember now the last time that anyone had dropped in.

George didn't find the supper disappointing at all. He was already finishing the soup and stuffing a rather large piece of bread into his mouth.

"This is wonderful," he said, between chews. "I haven't had

anything to eat since the day before yesterday."

Mouse was horrified to hear this. In fact, she was so concerned that she didn't notice until it was too late that George had put his hot soup bowl down on her polished table. She snatched it up with a cry. Sure enough, there was a white ring where the bowl had stood.

"Ooops, sorry," said George.

Mouse knew that she could not possibly send her visitor out into the blizzard again tonight. She hurried upstairs and made sure that the sheets on the spare-room bed were aired. She slipped a hot water bottle into the bed and ran back downstairs again to try to stop George doing any more damage to her furniture. She was too late.

"I am ever so sorry," said George. "I don't know how it happened. One minute I was rocking myself gently in your chair and the next minute the leg fell off. It must have been a little loose, I think."

"Rocking?" said Mouse faintly. She looked up at the wall, and sure enough she could see the mark where the chair had been bumped over and over again. This mouse would bring her home down about her ears if he carried on at this rate!

Nevertheless, Mouse clenched

her paws and asked George if he
would like a bath before bed.

"That would be bliss," said
George. "I haven't had a bath
since…"

"Yes, yes, that's all right," said
Mouse hurriedly. She really didn't
feel she could cope with the news
George had been about to give her.

Five minutes later, Mouse, doing
her best to tidy up downstairs,
heard George singing at the top of
his voice. It was a very silly song,
and he wasn't remotely in tune, but
still she caught herself smiling. It
was such a long time since she had
heard anyone really enjoying
themselves in her house.

But Mouse's smile was not in place for long. She began to wonder what state the bathroom would be in when George had finished, and just then … *splosh!* … a drop of water bounced off her nose.

Mouse looked up in horror. There was no doubt about it, water was dripping through her beautiful ceiling and on to her sofa below.

Mouse hurried up the stairs and banged furiously on the bathroom door.

"W-w-w-what?" came a voice, after a moment. "Oh no! Oh, I am sorry. I dozed off for a moment and left the taps running. There's not much water on the floor though. Honestly, there isn't."

"That's because it's on the floor downstairs," muttered Mouse to herself, but she felt sorry for the little mouse who was so tired he had almost drowned himself.

A moment later, George appeared at the bathroom door, wearing a pair of Mouse's late father's pyjamas. He looked clean and scrubbed, but his eyelids were drooping, and he had one paw on the door frame to support himself as he said goodnight to his hostess.

"Goodnight," said Mouse. "I hope you sleep well."

It took Mouse another three

hours to finish clearing up the sitting room *and* the bathroom, but then her standards were very high. She was exhausted herself when she finally tottered up the stairs to bed. And that is why she fell asleep the moment her head touched the pillow and didn't wake up at the crack of dawn as usual in the morning.

In fact, Mouse woke up feeling rather happy with the world. It took a few seconds for her to realise that this was because the smell of a fried breakfast and freshly brewed acorn coffee was wafting up the stairs.

Mouse sat up in bed. Someone

was in her kitchen! Then the events of the night before came flooding back. Oh no! *George* was in her kitchen, and what was more, he was *cooking*!

Mouse flew out of bed and into her dressing gown. Her little feet hardly touched the stairs as she rushed towards the kitchen. One glimpse was enough to tell her that it was even worse than she had feared. There was George, his

whiskers singed, flapping a tea towel at a flaming pan, while water running into the sink overflowed on to the floor. A second glimpse showed her two broken cups and a fish slice bent in two. And surely that wasn't … oh no, it couldn't be … that wasn't a *pancake* stuck to the ceiling? Mouse had to sit down in a hurry, and the floor was the nearest place.

"Oh, there you are," called George cheerfully. "I was just making you a little breakfast to thank you for being so kind. If you just wait there while I deal with this little fire, it will be ready for you in just a minute."

Mouse put her head in her hands. George was going to have to go, and he was going to have to go *soon*. She felt that every second that George spent in her house was another opportunity for disaster to strike.

But just at that moment, the visitor pushed a plate of pancakes and syrup under her nose. Much to Mouse's surprise, it smelt *delicious*! With all the excitement the night before, she remembered, she hadn't had any supper herself. Now she was too hungry to do anything other than pick up a spoon and start eating. And the pancakes tasted as delicious as they looked. How extraordinary!

As she munched her way through the pancakes, Mouse became aware that her visitor was talking.

"… so that's why I felt I just had to come and see her," he was saying. "I've heard so many stories about how kind she is to everyone, and how animals flock to see her when they are in trouble. Aunt

Petunia sounds such a wonderful person. I don't suppose you know her, do you? She lives somewhere around here. In fact, I'm sure you two must be friends, for you are just as kind as she is. *Do* you know her, Mouse?"

Mouse had the strangest feeling in her tail and whiskers. Petunia! That was a name she hadn't heard for so long. For the first time in years, Mouse knew what her real name was. No wonder George had looked and sounded familiar. He was her own sister Salvia's son.

If Mouse hadn't been sitting down already, she would have done so now. Instead, she asked George if she could have some of his acorn coffee.

Huddled in her dressing gown, Mouse sipped the excellent coffee and thought hard. There *had* been a time when she cared more for others than for herself. What had happened? Mouse looked around her home. In recent years, she had cared more for cleaning and tidying than for anything that was really important. Mouse felt ashamed. How could she confess who she was to this eager young mouse, when the evidence was all too plain that she only ever thought about her perfect home.

Then Mouse began to laugh.

The evidence wasn't plain at all!
Her kitchen was in ruins. The
sitting room ceiling was soggy.
There were marks on the walls and
furniture, and she hadn't even
looked to see what George had
done to the spare room.

Mouse looked again at her
nephew. He was certainly a
wonderful cook. He just needed a
little guidance about safety and
damage control. Mouse felt warmed
by the idea that George might have
to stay for a few weeks, months or
even years, so that she could help
him.

For the first time in ages,
Mouse felt really happy, and that

made her laugh too, especially as the flood on the floor was now creeping up her dressing gown.

"George," she smiled, "there's quite a lot I need to tell you…"

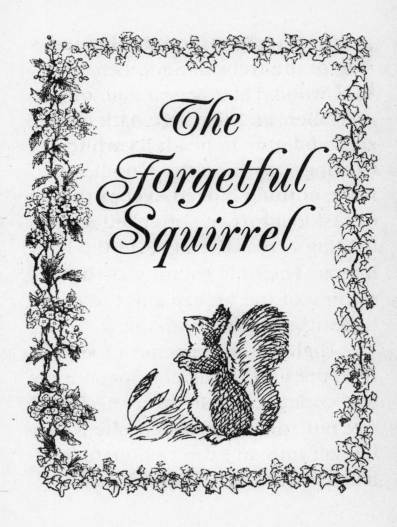

The Forgetful Squirrel

SNOW GLITTERED on the branches of the trees in Southfield Wood. Their leaves had long ago fallen, and the bare bark looked cold and grey beneath its white frosting. Down on the woodland floor, nothing moved except the occasional brown shrivelled leaf, drifting across the moss in the light breeze. The only sound was the sighing of the breeze and the far-off barking of a hungry fox.

High in the branches of an oak tree, the little squirrel slept soundly. She could not really hear the fox's cry, but still, in her sleep, she rolled herself into an even tighter, furry ball and tucked her little paws under her chin. She had made herself a cosy nest of twigs and leaves, as round as a ball. Inside, she was safe from the cold winds and the drifting snow.

The squirrel had been asleep since the first really cold day of winter. Once or twice, on a very sunny day, her little nose had twitched, and she had peeped out of her nest, or drey. But it was always too cold to go hunting for something to eat. Besides, she had spent the summer and autumn filling her tummy with all her favourite foods, so that she would be able to sleep through the winter without a single dinner.

The little squirrel slept on through the cold months. Elsewhere in the wood, other little creatures were fast asleep as well. Meanwhile, underground, the first stirrings of life began as tiny shoots started to make their long journey to the surface.

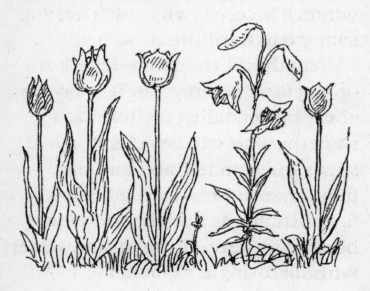

At last there came a day when the sunshine was quite warm on the branches. The snow had long ago melted away, and the sky had changed from grey to a watery blue.

The next day, the sun was even warmer, and it shone for a few minutes longer. Spring was well and truly on its way.

In her cosy drey, the little squirrel stirred. She felt the warmth of the sun trickling through the twigs and leaves of her treetop home. And she felt, too, that her tummy was just a tiny bit empty.

Poking her nose through the bottom of her nest, the little squirrel looked around at the waking world.

Far below, the first green shoots were showing under the trees. A few little animals were scurrying about among the roots and moss. The little squirrel wondered what she could find to eat so early in the year. Then she remembered something very important. Many months ago, when the nut-trees had been bowed down with shiny brown nuts, she had gathered dozens and dozens of them and stored them away for a morning just like this.

With a little chuckle, the squirrel clambered out of her nest and ran lightly along the branch. When it came to tree-climbing, she was an expert. Her clever little paws grasped the branches, while her big furry tail helped her to balance as she leapt without hesitation from branch to branch. However high she climbed, the little squirrel felt no fear. The treetops were her home, and she was happy there.

But the little squirrel had not hidden her nuts in the treetops. She had dug several little holes in the ground and buried her store here and there in the forest. Now all she had to do was to find one of these stores and enjoy her first meal of the year.

The little squirrel skipped happily down the trunk of the tree and looked around. She knew that one of her secret hiding places was not very far.

But, oh dear, how different things looked after the winter snows. The little squirrel remembered that her store was near a small bush with bright red and orange leaves. But now the leaves had all disappeared. Every bush was a mass of bare twigs. It was impossible to tell them apart.

Then the little squirrel remembered something else. There had been some red and white spotted toadstools near her hiding place. She looked eagerly around, but the clump of toadstools had also disappeared.

For the first time, the little squirrel began to feel worried. What if she couldn't find any of her nuts? What would she eat? How could she survive until spring had properly arrived?

All too soon, the light began to fade. Knowing that it would soon be cold and dark, the little squirrel hurried back to her home, where she could curl up, warm and safe, until morning.

"I'll worry about where my nut-store is then," she said to herself. "Tonight I will have a good sleep, so that I am ready to search tomorrow."

But in the morning, the little squirrel had no more idea where she had stored her food than she had had the night before.

"Perhaps I will be able to see where the ground has been disturbed," thought the little squirrel. But even as the thought crossed her mind, she recalled vividly how carefully she had patted the earth back into place after each burial.

"I have been too clever," said

the little squirrel. "What am I going to do?"

All day long, the hungry creature scampered through the wood. She was so worried about her food-stores now that she was not very careful to look out for danger. That is why, as she bounded around the base of a mighty oak tree, she came face to face with a long, lean, reddish creature. It was the fox!

Now foxes do not often catch squirrels, for they are not good climbers, but no hungry fox is going to give up the chance of supper when it comes leaping towards him. With one swift

movement, the fox caught hold of the little squirrel's tail in his strong jaws.

"Where are you off to?" he asked between clenched teeth.

"I'm … I'm … I'm searching for my food-stores," said the little squirrel in a rush. The poor little animal was so frightened that she said the first thing that came into her head, which happened to be the truth.

"Food-stores?" queried the fox, for at least one of those words was of very great interest to him at the moment. "And what might be in these food-stores?"

"Oh, um, rabbits," said the

squirrel, thinking as fast as she could. "Rabbits and chickens and one or two ducks."

The very mention of those creatures made the fox's mouth water. They were much more to his liking than squirrel, which in fact he had never tasted.

"And where exactly are these food-stores?" he enquired.

The little squirrel had her wits about her now.

"They are here somewhere," she said. "But I can't quite remember which tree I hid them under. It will take me weeks to find them, but with your strong paws and digging expertise, you will be able to unearth them in a few minutes. I think that this tree is the best place to start."

The fox had begun digging before he had even had a chance to think about what the squirrel had said. Somehow the mention of chickens and rabbits and ducks had muddled his usually sharp brain.

The digging was much slower than usual because the fox had to keep a tight grip on the squirrel's tail, but before long he had dug quite a deep hole under the oak tree.

There was nothing there at all.

"Then it might be this tree," said the squirrel, pointing to a nearby trunk.

The fox felt that he had very little to lose. After all, if he did not find the food-store, at least he had a plump little squirrel for his supper.

But the second hole was empty as well.

"One more," growled the fox between his teeth, "and then I'm going to eat you!"

The fox began to dig his third hole, and it did not take him long to come upon a whole mass of little round, brown shiny objects.

The fox could not believe his eyes. He felt a great anger rising up inside him and he opened his mouth in a mighty shout.

"NUTS?" he bellowed. "What good are nuts to ME?"

But, of course, when he opened his mouth, the little squirrel was able to jump free, and in ten seconds flat, she had scampered to the top of the nearest tree.

"They're terribly good for you!" she called down cheekily. "A nut a day keeps the doctor away, that's what I always say."

The fox was absolutely furious. He chased his tail round and round the tree to relieve his feelings. Then he sat down to wait with a very determined expression on his foxy face.

"Little squirrel," he called, "I'm going to wait here until you come down. You can't stay up there for ever."

"No," called the squirrel, "but I can jump to another tree, just look at me!" And spreading her beautiful tail out behind her, she leapt across the clearing to the tree opposite.

Now, the fox could not sit at the bottom of every tree in the wood, and anyway, his tummy, which had been empty, now felt as hollow as a cave. Muttering fiercely, he slunk away in search of food.

As for the little squirrel, she had found her first food-store — or at least the fox had. She ran down the tree and quickly gathered up as many nuts as she could carry.

The squirrel never did find all her stores, but the nuts she hid and lost grew into new nut-trees, so they fed her daughters and her granddaughters. And they were much better at remembering things, I'm happy to say.

Good Neighbours

RUDDINGTON BUNNY lived a quiet life. Every morning, after breakfast, he tidied his house. Then he read the newspaper. Sometimes he played chess with his friend Ashby Squirrel. In the afternoon, he did his shopping. And in the evening, there was nothing Ruddington liked better than a cup of blackberry tea by the fire, and a good book to read.

Ruddington enjoyed his life. Everything about it seemed absolutely perfect — until the day Scarrington Owl moved into the house just above Ruddington's.

Oh, Scarrington was friendly enough. And he was kind and

generous and kept his house tidy.
He was a good neighbour. In fact,
thought Ruddington, Scarrington
Owl would have been a perfect
neighbour if it hadn't been for one
thing.

Scarrington was noisy!

Every night, just about the time
Ruddington was getting ready for
bed, Scarrington Owl was just
waking up. And when Ruddington
was snuggled down under the
covers, all set to drift off to
dreamland, Scarrington began to
hoot.

"Hoo-hoo-hooooo," Scarrington
hooted. "Hoo-hoo-HOOOOO! Hoo-
hoo-HOOOOOO-hoooo-hoo!" On

and on it went, all through the night. Poor Ruddington tossed and turned and just couldn't get any sleep at all.

"I'll have to do something," Ruddington muttered one night. Wearily, he stumbled out of bed and went to the window.

"Please keep your voice down," he shouted out of the open window.

But Scarrington was hooting so loudly, he didn't hear.

In desperation, Ruddington went to his broom cupboard and got out his long-handled mop. Ruddington banged the mop handle hard against the ceiling. BANG! BANG! BANG! Scarrington hooted even louder.

"I'll have to go up there myself," muttered Ruddington, putting on his dressing gown as quickly as he could.

So upstairs Ruddington Bunny climbed, and he knocked on Scarrington's door.

"Excuse me," he said, when Scarrington answered his knock, "but it's two in the morning, and I'm trying to get to sleep. Do you think you could hoot just a little less loudly?"

"Oh dear," said Scarrington. "I'm ever so sorry for the disturbance. I'll try to keep the noise down."

"Thank you," said Ruddington, stumbling back downstairs. He was so tired that he was almost asleep before he got back into his bed.

For the next two nights, Scarrington's hooting was a bit softer, and Ruddington thought his sleepless nights were a thing of the past. But on the third night, the hooting got louder, and on the fourth night, it was louder still. By the end of the week, things were just as bad as they ever were.

"I'm sorry," said Scarrington, when Ruddington came to see him again. "Owls just have to hoot at night. It's what we do, and the louder we can do it, the better. I'm afraid you'll just have to put up with it. After all, we are neighbours, and neighbours have to

learn to live with one another, don't they?"

When Ashby came to visit the next morning, Ruddington said, "I'm sorry, but I'm just too tired to play chess today."

"Is it your noisy neighbour again?" asked Ashby looking sympathetically at his friend.

"Yes," wailed Ruddington. "I don't know what to do!"

"Why not try wearing earmuffs to bed?" suggested Ashby. "That's what I did when the moles who live downstairs from me had triplets. The babies cried and cried every night, but I never heard a thing."

It was worth a try, thought Ruddington. So that afternoon he went out and bought a pair of thick, fluffy earmuffs.

But a bunny needs very big earmuffs, and they made poor

Ruddington terribly hot and uncomfortable. In the end, he had to take them off.

One day, Ruddington's cousin Bingham Bunny came to visit.

"I once lived next door to a family of very rowdy hedgehogs," said Bingham. "I put pillows on my walls, and that muffled the noise. Maybe that would work for you, too."

So that evening, Ruddington taped some pillows to his ceiling. Bingham was right — it did muffle the noise, and Ruddington fell into a deep, contented sleep.

But in the middle of the night, the pillows fell down.

Ruddington woke with a start

— and a whole mouthful of feathers!

"It's no use," Ruddington said to himself the next morning. "I will just have to move house. It's the only way I will ever have any peace and quiet again."

Ruddington was all set to go out and see if there were any houses for rent, and had started to think about just what kind of home he would be looking for, when the post came through the door. Among the circulars and the bills, there was a very fancy envelope address-ed to him, and when he opened it, he was certainly most surprised.

The card inside said:

You are invited to
a musical evening presented by

THE OWL OPERATIC SOCIETY

at the home of
Scarrington Owl

7:00 PM tonight Refreshments will be served

So, at seven o'clock precisely, Ruddington Bunny climbed the stairs to Scarrington's house. He was pleased to see that Ashby and Cousin Bingham were both there, as well as lots of other friends and neighbours. And all the owls of the forest were there, dressed in their very best outfits. There was a long table, spread with delicious things to eat and drink, and everyone seemed in a festive mood.

After a few minutes, Scarrington cleared his throat. "Ladies and gentlemen," he announced. "Please be seated. Our recital is about to begin."

Everyone sat down, and the owls gathered together at the front of the room, standing very smartly in rows.

"Hoo-hoo-hoo-hooo," sang Scarrington, to give the others the key — and the singing began.

It was magnificent! All hooting in harmony, the owls sang their way through dozens of wonderful songs. They sang slow, romantic, sentimental songs, and quick, bright, funny songs. They even sang loud songs and soft ones, happy songs and sad ones. They even took requests and sang special favourites — and everyone joined in the choruses. As the moon rose, and stars twinkled in sky, the music of happy voices filled the forest.

Much later, as dawn broke, the singing finally came to an end, and everyone prepared to fly, scamper, shuffle and hop home. Before he left, Ruddington went up to Scarrington.

"Thank you so much for inviting me," he said. "I can't remember when I've had so much fun! And now that I know how delightful your hooting can be, I'm sure it won't bother me any more."

"I'm glad you had a good time," said Scarrington. "And I have some special news for you."

"Oh?" said Ruddington.

"Yes," said Scarrington Owl. "There's no need for you to worry about the noise any longer. The Owl Operatic Society has found a splendid new rehearsal hall. Starting tomorrow, you'll be glad to know that we'll be practising our hooting and singing in our very own tree."

"But you're not moving away?" asked Ruddington, anxiously.

"Of course not!" exclaimed Scarrington. "This tree will always be my home."

"Oh, I'm glad," said Ruddington Bunny. "Because, you know, you've become much more than a neighbour — you're also a very special friend!"

The Sleepy Teddy Bear

ADAM HAD a beautiful teddy bear called Mr Muffle. He had lovely golden fur and two bright little eyes. Adam's grandmother thought he looked a little chilly one winter's day, so she knitted him a bright red sweater. Adam felt that he was a very special teddy bear indeed.

Mr Muffle had lots of jobs to do. He kept an eye on things in Adam's room during the day, when Adam was out and about. He warmed up Adam's bed in the evening, ready for him to jump into after his bath. And *just* before Adam got into bed, Mr Muffle had his most important task of all. He had to check under the bed for *monsters*. Adam had once read a story about a monster who lived under a little boy's bed. The more he read about it, the more likely it seemed to him that the fluffy, dark space under his bed was just the kind of place that a monster might love to live. And you never knew when a monster might move in. That was why Mr Muffles had to look under the bed *every* night.

When Mr Muffles had checked very carefully under the bed (and had a quick look behind the curtains as well, just to be on the safe side), Adam was happy to cuddle down between the sheets and go to sleep. He didn't need his bedroom door to be a ajar or a night light on his bedside table. He knew that he was as safe as he could be with Mr Muffles beside him.

One evening in late autumn, when it was already dark outside, Adam's mother looked at the clock and told him it was time for his bath and bed. Adam was in the middle of playing with his new space game, so he pretended not to hear her.

"Adam!" called his mother. "I know you can hear me, even on Mars. Put your toys away now and get ready for bed. We're already quite late this evening."

"All right, Mum," said Adam, reluctantly. He really didn't feel like going to bed yet. As he was putting the pieces of his space game back in the box, one of them rolled under the table, and Adam gave it another nudge with his foot.

"Mum," he said, "I can't go yet. I've lost one of the pieces of my game. I must find it before I go to bed or … or … I won't be able to sleep because I'll be worried."

"All right," sighed Adam's mother, and she got down on her hands and knees to help him look for the missing piece.

It took quite a long time to find the piece under the table, partly because Adam managed to "search" between his mother and the table most of the time, but at last it was found.

"Now hurry up!" said Mum. "It's

an hour past your bedtime. Just a quick bath, Adam, and no more delays please."

Adam felt a little bit guilty as he scampered up the stairs. He thought for a moment about "losing" one of the ducks from his bath, but he was beginning to be quite tired now.

The sleepy boy had his bath in double-quick time. I'm pretty sure that there were lots of parts of him that were not much cleaner after his bath than they were before it. (Adam never was very keen on washing his *ears*, for example!)

When Adam went into his bedroom, he knew at once that

something was different. In fact, something was more than different — it was *wrong*! It took him a moment to realise what the problem was.

Mr Muffles was asleep! Yes, the teddy bear in the red sweater was sitting in his usual place on the bed, but there was no doubt about it, those bright little beady eyes were closed. A tiny snoring sound came from Mr Muffles' furry chest.

Adam climbed into bed and clutched Mr Muffles, who did not wake up.

"Goodnight!" said Adam's mother from the doorway. "Go straight to sleep now! And goodnight, Mr Muffles!"

"But Mum!" called Adam. "Mr Muffles is already asleep!"

"I'm not surprised," said his mother. "Have you seen what the time is? All boys and their bears should be fast asleep by now. Goodnight!"

Well, Adam settled down into his bed. He felt more sleepy than ever, but every time he closed his eyes, a worrying thought would pop into his mind.

Mr Muffles hadn't checked under the bed. What if there was something green and hairy under there, just waiting until he was asleep? Or, worse still, what if there was something purple and slimy under there, ready to ooze across the carpet as soon as the coast was clear? Or what about something brown and prickly, with very sharp teeth?

Adam could feel a tingling at the tips of his toes, just where a monster might decide to nibble first on its midnight snack.

Adam gave Mr Muffles a little shake. "Wake up!" he whispered. "Mr Muffles! Wake up!" But the silly old teddy bear just carried on sleeping.

Adam tried very hard to be sensible. "There was no monster under the bed last night," he said to himself, "and no monster the night before that, *or* the night before that. In fact, there has *never* been a monster under the bed, so there won't be one now."

Still, at the back of his mind, a little voice was saying, "You don't *know* that there isn't a monster tonight, because nobody has checked to see. And it *would* be the very night that nobody checked when a monster might come."

Adam lay awake in the darkness and listened very carefully. He was almost sure he could hear a sort of scrabbling, scratching, snorting sound coming from you-know-where. And wasn't that a slobbering, squelching, sucking kind of noise, coming from somewhere down by his toes?

Adam decided to be brave. He switched on the bedside light and got out of bed. If Mr Muffles had the courage to look under the bed, then so did he.

First Adam rummaged in his chest of drawers for his torch. It was true that Mr Muffles didn't use a torch, but then bear eyes are much sharper than human ones, as everyone knows.

Adam found his torch and turned it on. He knelt down very quietly and took a deep breath.

What was best? To snatch up the corner of the quilt and have one quick look? Or to lift the quilt gently, gently and very slowly peep under the bed? Adam couldn't make up his mind. Mr Muffles did one quick look, but then he was used to the job. Adam felt that a beginner should perhaps move more slowly — to make sure he did the job thoroughly, of course.

So very, very slowly, Adam bent down, and very, very gently, he lifted up the corner of his quilt. Bending closer, he peered into the space under the bed, into the dusty dark.

"Aaaaaaaagh!" yelled Adam, as he realised what he was seeing.

"Aaaaaaaagh!" yelled the monster, blinking its yellow eyes.

Yes, there *was* a monster under the bed, and it looked just as frightened as Adam was!

Now all the time that Adam had been getting ready to look under the bed, he had only half believed there might be a monster. If you had asked him to say whether, in his heart of hearts, he really

thought there was a monster under his bed, then he would have said, "No, of course not. No one *really* has monsters *anywhere*."

But here he was, face to face with a monster. Adam rubbed his eyes. The easiest reason for seeing a monster might be that he was already asleep. But Adam was awake all right. He was particularly sure after he had rubbed his eyes, because he had forgotten that he was still holding the torch and he managed to clonk himself on the forehead with it.

"Oooooh!" said the monster, sympathetically.

Adam smiled. It was really quite

a friendly looking monster, even if it did have green spots and funny purple hair.

The monster smiled. He had a lot of rather sharp-looking little teeth, but then so do kittens, and everyone thinks *they* are cute.

"I'm a monster," said the monster, "in case you didn't realise." He had quite a high-pitched, squeaky little voice.

"I'm Adam," said Adam. "I'm a boy," he added, in case the monster wasn't very used to humans. "Er ... have you lived here long?"

"Oh, a few months now," said the monster carelessly. "It's a very nice bed to live under. The last one

I had was always being swept and cleaned. You know, there is nothing in the world that monsters hate more than vacuum cleaners. Ugh!"

"What else is under there?" asked Adam curiously, peering past the monster.

"Well, now, this is my private place, so I think that's *my* business," said the monster, primly. "But if you're thinking about that football sock you lost, yes, it is here, and no, you can't have it back."

"All right," said Adam. "I've got some new ones now, anyway."

Adam tried to think what his next question should be, but really he had so many, he hardly knew where to begin. Then he thought of something that was really quite important. The trouble was, it was quite a delicate matter, too.

"I was wondering," said Adam, "whether you have everything you need under there. You know, food and so on?"

"You want to know if I'm going to eat you," said the monster, with a nasty little giggle but a rather nice smile.

"Well, I did wonder," said Adam, trying to look as if he didn't mind very much one way or the other. "What *do* monsters eat these days?"

The monster giggled again. "Don't worry," he said, "I survive very nicely on the odd spider that crawls down the corner. Delicious!"

Adam felt a little better after that, but it didn't seem right, somehow, just to get back into bed and go to sleep. He wondered if he really would be able to sleep, *knowing* that there was a monster under the bed, however friendly it was.

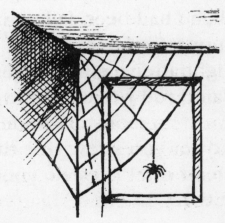

Just then, Adam heard a little snuffling sound. It was Mr Muffles, waking up at last! With a soft thud, Mr Muffles landed on the floor beside Adam. The sleepy teddy bear took in the situation at a glance.

"Ah," he said, "I see that you two have met."

Adam felt strongly that Mr Muffles had some explaining to do. After all, he had been failing in his most important job.

"Night after night, Mr Muffles," said Adam, "you promised me that there were no monsters under my bed. And yet you knew that there was at least one! How do you explain that?"

"Now, Adam," said Mr Muffles, trying to sound like an old and wise bear, "I never actually said that there were no monsters. *You* said, 'Is everything all right under the bed?' and I said, 'Yes!' As you can see, it was all right. It's just that there is a little tiny monster there as well."

"But how did you know it was all right?" asked Adam. "How did you know he wasn't a really very dangerous monster, who might crunch teddy bears and leave only their ears on the pillow in the morning?"

"*Please*, said Mr Muffles, "do give me credit for some sense. The monster and I have had some long chats while you were asleep. I was quite sure that no harm would come to us."

"And what do we do now?" asked Adam. "That's what I'd like to know."

"I can quite see," said Mr Muffles, "that from your point of view things are rather different now. Sleeping with a monster under the bed that you don't know is there is a very different matter from sleeping with a monster under the bed that you *do* know is there. Do you think you could ever get used to the idea, Adam?"

"I don't think so," said Adam. "It doesn't feel right, somehow."

"Very well," said Mr Muffles, then I have another idea.

If you were to creep into Adam's room tonight, you would see a very strange sight. Adam and the monster sleep *in* the bed, and

Adam finds that the monster is every bit as cuddly as Mr Muffles. The teddy bear sleeps *under* the bed, so that he can make sure that no new monsters try to take over the space during the night. During the day, they swap over.

So remember, a monster under the bed is not the end of the world, but do make sure your teddy bear is doing his job properly each night, won't you?

Mr Potter's Problem

I T WAS TWO O'CLOCK in the morning. As usual, Mr Potter was down in the kitchen, making himself a cup of tea. At two o'clock in the morning? Well, yes. You see Mr Potter simply couldn't sleep. Rather than lying awake, staring into the darkness, he felt it was better to come down and have a comforting cup of tea. At least from here he couldn't hear the dreadful noise.

You see, after thirty years of married life, Mr Potter's wife had started to snore. It wasn't just a gentle snuffling noise. It was an awful, trumpeting, elephant-on-the-warpath sort of noise. It was the kind of thing you couldn't sleep through no matter how hard you tried. And Mr Potter had tried very hard indeed.

The first thing he had tried was Mind over Matter. If I just pretend I can't hear it, he thought, I *won't* hear it, and I'll be able to get back to sleep.

Well, I don't know if you've ever *tried* to sleep through a deafening elephant-on-the-warpath trumpeting noise, but it's not very easy. Just as the echo of the snore is dying away, and you are drifting off to sleep again, an ear-splitting blast hits you amidships.

Mr Potter was a practical man,

so the next thing he tried was Double Strength Ear Plugs. The label on the packet claimed that you could sleep through a hurricane

with this wonderful product in place. Well, maybe you could, but you couldn't sleep through Mrs Potter's snoring, as Mr Potter can confirm. It was slightly softer, oh yes, and sort of muffled too, but in a way that was worse. With ear plugs in, Mr Potter felt as though the noise was inside his own head. It was really horrible.

Now you will be asking, why didn't Mr Potter do the sensible thing and hop off to spend the night in the spare room, where the snoring would sound like a faraway bugle call. Well, Mr Potter was a really kind man, and he was determined that his wife wouldn't find

out about her problem from *him*.
You see, Mrs Potter was a proud
and proper woman. She wouldn't
have dreamed of letting the next-
door neighbours see her in her
curlers or of wearing her slippers
in the street. Her kind husband
knew that she would be mortified
if she knew about the snoring, so
he was doing everything he could
to keep the news from her, but, oh
dear, the poor man was beginning
to feel faint from lack of sleep!

Mr Potter went to the library to
read up about the causes of
snoring. Before long he had a
whole pile of books open in front
of him. It seemed that there were

as many views about how to solve the problem as there were people who snored.

But one paragraph caught Mr Potter's eye. It claimed that a lack of fresh air could make matters worse.

That night, as they were getting ready for bed, Mr Potter said casually to his wife, "It's quite warm tonight, my dear. Do you mind if we have the window open a little? I read in the paper that it's terribly important to have plenty of fresh air when you get to our age."

"It's terribly important not to catch pneumonia too," said his wife, "but I suppose it *isn't* very cold tonight, so if you'd like the window open, that's fine."

Mr Potter smiled to himself as he opened the window wide. Maybe this would do the trick.

Fifteen minutes later, Mr Potter was off to make an early cup of tea. The noise seemed *worse*! He was so tired that he actually nodded off at the kitchen table ... and woke up five hours later with a stiff neck, just in time to crawl back to bed for another couple of hours of elephants.

Next morning, Mr Potter took himself off to the park for a brisk walk to clear his head. While he was gone, there came a knock at the door. When Mrs Potter went to answer it, she found her next-door neighbour looking embarrassed on the doorstep.

"Excuse me, Mrs Potter," said Mrs Maybury. "I wonder if I could have a word? It's a rather delicate matter, so perhaps I could come inside?"

"By all means," said Mrs Potter, who certainly didn't want the world and his wife knowing her business.

When the two ladies were sitting comfortably in the living room, Mrs Maybury seemed to be having some difficulty in knowing where to begin.

"Are you feeling quite well?" asked Mrs Potter. "You look pale."

"The fact is," said Mrs Maybury, grateful for a place to start, "I haven't had a wink of sleep all night. That's why I've come."

Mrs Potter was puzzled. "I'm not sure how I can help," she said slowly.

"You see, the reason I can't sleep," confessed Mrs Maybury, "is your husband."

Mrs Potter almost fell out of her chair. For one wild moment she imagined that Mrs Maybury had taken a fancy to Mr Potter and was unable to sleep for thinking of him. Then she pulled herself together and realised she was being ridiculous.

Mr Potter was a dear, sweet man, and the love of her life, but he was hardly the stuff that dreams are made of.

"I shall have to ask you to explain," said Mrs Potter rather stiffly to her neighbour.

"Oh, please don't be angry," cried Mrs Maybury, hearing Mrs Potter's tone. "I know it's embarrassing, but we have lived next door to each other for twelve years now. We should be able to talk about these things like mature human beings."

"But what things?" asked Mrs

Potter, feeling as though she was wading through treacle.

"Why, Mr Potter's *snoring*," said Mrs Maybury.

Mrs Potter was more surprised than she would have been if Mrs Maybury *had* conceived a passion for Mr Potter.

"His snoring?" she gasped.

"Yes," moaned Mrs Maybury. "We hear it every night, you know. The walls are quite thick between our houses. I never hear your television or your vacuum cleaner or anything. But that snoring positively shakes the walls! We've been hearing it for some time, but it wasn't loud enough to disturb us, and I didn't like to say anything. Last night was the final straw. I think you had your window open, and we did too. It was deafening! I lay awake all night, and so did my husband."

"Indeed?" said Mrs Potter coldly. She didn't take kindly to criticism, and Mrs Maybury was beginning to annoy her. "I can truthfully say that it has never disturbed *me*," she went on, "but then I am a sound sleeper, not *foolishly nervous* or worried by *silly little things*. I do realise that not everyone has my excellent health and clear conscience."

"Well, I did feel I should mention it," said Mrs Maybury, rising to her feet.

"And I'm very glad you did so," said Mrs Potter warmly. "I do hope it has helped you to get it off your chest, my dear."

Mrs Potter showed her neighbour to the door, and Mrs Maybury, feeling oddly as though it was *she* who had the problem, hurried home to report to her husband that the meeting had not been an unqualified success.

As soon as she had closed the front door, Mrs Potter picked up the telephone and got to work. She knew perfectly well that her neighbour was a truthful woman, and she didn't doubt for a moment that what she had said was true, although it certainly was extraordinary that she herself had never been woken by Mr Potter's snoring. Mrs Potter was taking no chances. She didn't want any more neighbours coming round to complain, and she wasn't going to run the risk of her own sleep being disturbed, now that she knew about Mr Potter's "Little Problem".

By the time her husband came home from his walk, Mrs Potter had made her plans and was ready to put them into action. She made Mr Potter a cup of tea and asked him to sit down as she had something serious to say.

"Now, Alfred," she said, "you

know that I've never been one to beat about the bush. I like to call a spade a spade. The fact is that the neighbours have been complaining about your snoring, so I've had to *take steps*. I've ordered a double-glazing firm to start work tomorrow, and, as I really can't afford to lose my sleep, I wondered if you could stay in the spare room until your little problem is better. I do realise you can't help it, dear."

Mr Potter opened his mouth to protest. Then he realised that his problems were at an end.

"Of course, dear," he said.

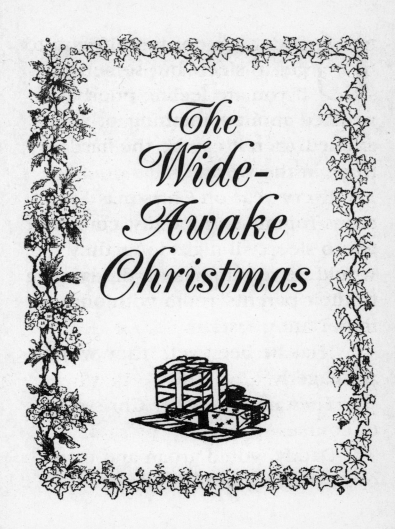

The Wide-Awake Christmas

USUALLY, it's not too difficult to get to sleep, but sometimes, if you are feeling poorly, or worried about something, or very excited, then it can be the hardest thing in the world.

Every year on Christmas Eve, twins Tommy and Joe just could not get to sleep. All night long, they would be running along the landing to their parents' room with one important question.

"Has he been yet?" they would ask eagerly.

They meant Father Christmas, of course.

Daddy would groan and turn over. Mummy would call out.

"Go back to bed, Tommy and Joe. You'll be so tired in the morning, you won't be able to stay awake to open your presents *if* Father Christmas brings you any. I don't know what he'll have to say about two such naughty little boys."

"Oh, don't tell him! Don't tell him! We'll be good!" cried Tommy and Joe.

"We don't have to tell him," growled Daddy. "He knows *everything*. You just watch out."

And the twins would scamper back to bed and try ever so hard to shut their eyes and fall asleep. But it was *so* difficult.

Twenty minutes later, there

would be little feet skipping across the landing again and right into Mummy's and Daddy's big bedroom.

"Has he been yet?" the little boys would whisper, tugging at the quilt.

"He *did* come," their father would whisper back, "but he heard that two bad little boys were not asleep, so he went away again. He *may* come back, but only if you shut your eyes and *keep* them shut."

As fast as their little legs would carry them, the boys would hurry back to their beds. But did they go straight to sleep until morning? Oh no. Ten minutes later they were off again. This time the question was different.

"Is it morning yet?" asked Joe.

Daddy muttered and mumbled and sat right up in bed.

"Do *you* think it's morning?" he said, looking at the bedside light. Its hands were glowing in the dark. They said half past three.

"It might be," said Tommy, hopefully. "Then we can open our presents.

"It's *dark*," moaned Daddy. "It's the middle of the night. It's ages and ages and ages until morning. *Go* back to bed and don't come back until you can see that it's getting light outside. Do you understand, both of you?"

Tommy and Joe nodded their heads and went back to their room. But did they snuggle back into bed? Oh no. They stood on tiptoes so that they could see out of the window. They wanted to be ready the very *moment* it began to get light.

It was a pity that a tree blowing in the wind made the next-door neighbour's outside light come on only fifteen minutes later.

Mummy and Daddy were drifting back to sleep when ... *woomph!* ... *woomph!* ... two little bodies jumped right in the middle of their tummies.

"It's morning. It is! It is!" shouted the boys, bouncing up and down.

I'm afraid that what Daddy said then is really not repeatable. Luckily it was muffled by the quilt. Five seconds later, two little boys were being dragged unceremoniously across the landing and plonked ...*one!* ... *two!* ... in their beds.

"If I hear a peep out of either of you in the next three hours, I won't answer for my actions," yawned Daddy, pulling the curtains firmly shut and making the fiercest face he could.

What do you think happened? I won't go into the details, but by half past four, Mummy and Daddy had given up and were hugging cups of coffee in the sitting room, while two excited little boys opened a wonderful pile of presents.

Sometimes, you just have to give in gracefully.

When it was nearly time for the next Christmas, however, Daddy put his foot down.

"Now, I want a word with you

boys," he said. "You know we have Granny coming to stay with us this Christmas. She's an old lady, and she won't want to be woken up in the middle of the night. You could make her very ill. You are both big boys now, so I want you to promise me that you won't come out of your room until it is morning. You've got your own big teddy bear clock now. When the little hand is pointing straight down and the big hand is pointing straight up, you can get up. That's still very early, but it isn't the middle of the night. Now, is it a deal?"

"Yes, Daddy," said Joe.

"Yes, Daddy," said Tommy.

The boys loved their granny. They certainly wouldn't want to do anything to upset her.

To the twins' parents, it seemed as if Christmas Eve arrived far too quickly. To the boys, the days seemed to crawl past. But at last it

was here, and daddy went to collect Granny from the station.

"Happy Christmas, boys!" she called, as she came through the front door. Tommy and Joe couldn't help noticing that she had two bulging bags of presents and a suitcase that looked as if it was about to burst.

That evening, the whole family had a special Christmas Eve supper, with crackers and candles. The boys were almost unbearably excited.

"Now, it's bedtime for you two," said Mummy at last.

"Goodnight, boys," smiled Daddy. "Now, remember what I said, won't you?"

"Goodnight, darlings," said Granny. And, much to their surprise, she winked at them, careful that Daddy shouldn't see.

Tommy and Joe went to their bedroom and put on their pyjamas. They climbed into their beds and turned off the light. A few moments passed.

"Are you asleep?" whispered Tommy to his twin.

"No," whispered Joe, "are you?"

The boys lay staring into the darkness. They could just see the luminous hands of their teddy bear clock. It was *hours* until the hands would be pointing straight up and straight down.

Time passed *so* slowly. It almost seemed as though the hands of the clock were going backwards! There was no way that the boys could get to sleep.

"This is going to be a *long* night," groaned Joe.

Later still, the twins heard their parents saying goodnight to Granny on the landing. The little strip of light at the bottom of the door disappeared as the landing light was turned off. Then there was silence.

More long, long minutes passed. The house was very, very quiet. Then the boys heard a funny little rustling sound and a tiny squeak as someone turned the handle of their door.

"Are you awake, boys?" said Granny's voice quietly.

"No!' whispered the twins.

"Good!" said Granny, coming into the room. "I don't know about you, but I never can get to sleep on Christmas Eve. It's much too exciting. I thought perhaps we could open one or two little presents to make the time pass more quickly. But you've got to promise to be very, very quiet. We don't want to wake up you-know-who, *do* we?"

Well, Granny and the twins had a wonderful time. Some of the presents were games to play, and it was even more fun playing and trying to be as quiet as mice at the same time.

Granny had sensibly brought one or two little Christmas snacks as well.

"Just to keep us going," she giggled, opening a tin of sausage rolls and cheese straws.

Unfortunately, they were all three having such a good time, they didn't keep an eye on the clock. It was still dark when the big hand finally pointed straight up and the little hand pointed straight down.

Granny and the boys didn't notice the door silently opening.

"Mother!" cried Daddy. "You really are the limit!" But he was laugh-ing until tears streamed down his face.

"You know the worst thing?" said Daddy later, when they were all downstairs. "Granny would never have let *me* open my presents early, when I was little!"

"Well," smiled his mother, "that's why *grannies* have more fun."

The Bedtime Bunny

CAROLINE'S MOTHER shook her head firmly. "No," she said. "Not under any circumstances. Not tonight. Not tomorrow night. Not any night. Do you understand?"

Caroline opened her mouth to protest, but her mother had her I-will-not-change-my-mind-whatever-you-say face on, so she went meekly off to bed. It just wasn't fair.

The trouble was all about Caroline's fluffy white rabbit, Snowdrop. She wanted to take him to bed with her, but Mummy said it was out of the question. Poor Caroline, you are probably thinking. Why shouldn't she have her toy rabbit it bed with her? But Snowdrop wasn't a toy rabbit. He was real!

"Rabbits are cuddly and friendly, I know," Caroline's mother had said, "but, darling, they're not indoor animals. They belong outside. Snowdrop might make a terrible mess in your bedroom, and he really wouldn't be happy, you know."

Caroline was quite, quite sure her mother was wrong. Darling Snowdrop was always so pleased to see her when she went out to his hutch with a few green cabbage leaves.

He liked to play, too, when she let him out of his hutch for a hop around the garden. She had to be very careful that he didn't hop right away, but that wasn't because he didn't like her, that was because he was a very adventurous bunny.

Caroline sat in her bedroom and felt close to tears. It was a cold night, and she felt sure that Snowdrop would much rather be with her in her warm little bed. So do you know what that naughty

little girl did? She waited until she could hear that her mother was watching television downstairs, then she put on her slippers and dressing gown and crept out of the back door, taking her little torch with her.

Snowdrop seemed rather surprised to see her. Although the wind was whistling around his cage, he looked quite cosy and comfortable curled up in his pile of straw. In fact, when Caroline put her hands in to pick him up, he didn't really seem to want to come.

"You'll like it, Snowdrop, really you will," said the little girl. "But you mustn't make a noise as we go upstairs. All right?"

Caroline and her rabbit slipped through the back door and shut it carefully behind them. The little girl crept up the stairs as quietly as she could, which was quite difficult because Snowdrop would keep struggling. At last they were safely in Caroline's bedroom, with the door shut behind them.

Clutching her rabbit tightly, the little girl snuggled down in bed and stretched out her hand to turn off the light. It should have been lovely, drifting off to sleep with her cuddly bunny in her arms, but, oh dear, Snowdrop was the *wriggliest* rabbit you have ever come across. And he was quite strong too. He wriggled and he jiggled and in the end he kicked Caroline so hard with his big back feet that she said, "Oh!" and let go of him.

With a *thump!* Snowdrop landed on the floor. Caroline heard him hopping off towards her toy cupboard before she had a chance to turn on the light. Quickly, the little girl jumped out of bed and ran across the room to catch her rabbit.

"Come here, Snowdrop!" she called, as loudly as she dared. But Snowdrop was already knocking toys over and crashing around in the cupboard. Then he started to nibble the straw-stuffed paws of the little girl's favourite teddy bear!

Just then Mummy, who had been on her way upstairs and thought she heard a strange noise, popped her head round the door.

"Why is your light still on?" she asked. "Come on, darling. You've got school tomorrow."

Caroline swung round guiltily. She must make sure that her mother didn't see Snowdrop.

"I'm just getting into bed again, Mum," she said. "I just couldn't sleep because ... because ... because the wind was so loud."

Mummy looked at Caroline more suspiciously than she had done before. "No, it isn't," she said. "What's going on in here?"

"Nothing," said Caroline, but she couldn't help taking a quick look towards the cupboard.

Caroline's mother didn't need any more clues. She strode over to the cupboard and flung the doors wide open.

There was nothing to be seen. Mummy peered here and there, but she couldn't see anything strange. Caroline held her breath. Snowdrop was being so good and quiet.

Then Mummy frowned and wrinkled up her nose.

"What's that *smell*?" she asked. "Something in this cupboard smells extraordinarily like a ... fluffy ... white ... *rabbit*!"

Just at that moment, Snowdrop hopped right out of the cupboard, leaving the smell, a half-chewed teddy bear, a scratched toy train and a squashed puppet behind him. At first Mummy was really cross. Then she calmed down a little and said that she supposed there were some things that everyone just had to find out for themselves.

"Do you think Snowdrop was happy in your bed?" she asked.

"No," said Caroline.

"Do you think he was happy in your toy cupboard?"

"Well," said Caroline, "I think he did have quite a good time, yes, I do."

"And are *you* happy that he was in your toy cupboard?"

Caroline looked at the chewed teddy bear and damaged toys.

"No, not really," she whispered.

"Are you happy that you're going to have to clean everything in your cupboard and find out where that smell is coming from?" asked Mummy.

Caroline wrinkled her nose. "No, I'm not," she said.

"Are you happy that you didn't do what I said and told me stories when I came to see what was happening?"

"No." Caroline hung her head.

Mummy smiled and kissed her little girl.

"One more question, honey," she said.

"Where do you think rabbits really like to sleep?"

Caroline smiled. "In their hutches," she said, "outside."

I think she's right. Don't you?

The Dream Merchant

ONCE UPON A TIME, there was a little boy who had the most wonderful dreams. His name was David. Every night when he closed his eyes, it was as though he walked into a wonderful new world. But David's dreams didn't just come to him by chance. He bought them from the dream merchant, who visited him as soon as his eyes were closed. And the dream merchant had his price, as you will see.

It happened like this. One day, David had been rather lazy at school. He didn't pay attention during his lessons, and the teacher spoke to him sharply.

"Do you have nice dreams at

night, David?" she enquired, in front of the whole class.

"Sometimes," said David, looking puzzled.

"Then I'm surprised you need to dream during the day as well," said the teacher. "Perhaps your night-time dreams aren't exciting enough. I shall have to send the dream merchant to you."

Of course, all the children wanted to know what she meant, but the teacher just smiled mysteriously and would say nothing more.

That night, David went to bed as usual and fell asleep so quickly that he didn't even have time to turn his bedside lamp off.

"Good evening," said a magical voice in his ear.

David felt as though he was awake, although he knew he was really asleep.

"Good evening," he replied.

"I'm the dream merchant," said the voice. "A friend of mine told me that you might like a visit. What kind of dream would you like to have?"

"Isn't this already a dream?" asked David.

"Oh," said the dream merchant, "everything is a dream in a way. It depends how you look at it. Have you thought yet? What would you like to dream about tonight?"

"Could I dream about pirates?" asked David, who had been reading a very exciting book on just that subject.

"Of course," said the dream merchant. "Would you like an exciting dream, a scary dream, a comfortable dream, or a dream full of wonders?"

David wasn't sure. "I'd like an exciting dream," he said, "but could I have some … um … wonders as well?"

"No, no, only one kind at a time. You can have wonders tomorrow night if you like. An exciting dream it is. Now, what would you like to pay?"

"Pay?" echoed David. "What do you mean?"

"Well, I'm a merchant," said the magical voice a little impatiently. "I don't *give* things away, you know. I need something from you in return."

"What kind of something?" asked David.

"A whole day of paying attention at school, or a whole week of doing what your mother says, or a whole

month of making your bed properly. Which shall it be?"

David didn't hesitate. "I'll pay attention at school tomorrow," he said. With that, David heard a *woosh!* and a *whizz!* and he found himself on the deck of a pirate ship.

When David woke the next morning, he found that his lamp was still on, with his pirate book lying beside it. His head was spinning from the amazing adventures he had had during the night.

That day at school, he started work on his pirate project, and the teacher was delighted with the way he concentrated and had such imaginative ideas.

"It's exciting, isn't it?" she said, but whether she meant the project or the visit of the dream merchant, David wasn't sure.

After that, the dream merchant came every night. In exchange for marvellous dreams, David helped his father in the garden and stopped teasing his little sister.

He continued to pay attention at school. He was surprised to find that everything seemed to work a hundred times better when he just tried a tiny bit harder. And so it was that a night came when the dream merchant visited as usual.

David asked for a dream about castles, and the dream merchant was happy to oblige. But when it came to thinking of a suitable payment, there was a problem. Everything the dream merchant suggested was something that David did already.

"You know," said David. "I've learnt that doing my best at things makes me happier all the time. I do it anyway, even if I don't have a dream to pay for."

"Then I think my work is done," said the dream merchant, with a smile in his voice. "From now on, you can make your own dreams. In fact, most of the time you can do anything at all that you want to do. You just have to try, that's all."

You could try it too. It's true!

Bobby's
Best
Birthday
Present

IT WAS the morning of Bobby's birthday and he was very excited. When he came down to breakfast, there on the table was a big pile of presents. Bobby opened them one by one. There was a beautiful book with pictures of wild animals, a toy racing car and a baseball cap.

Bobby was very pleased with his presents, but where was the present from his parents? "Close your eyes and hold out your hands!" said his mother. When he opened his eyes there was a large rectangular parcel in his hands. Bobby tore off the wrapping and inside was a box. And inside the box was a wonderful, shiny, electric train set.

For a moment, Bobby looked at the train set lying in the box. It was so lovely he could hardly bear to touch it. There was an engine and six carriages all lying neatly on their

sides. Bobby carefully lifted the engine out of the box. Then he set up the track and soon he had the train whizzing round his bedroom floor. Freddie the cat came in and watched the train going round. Round and round she watched it go, then one time when the train came past her she swiped at it with her paw and derailed it. The engine and the six carriages came tumbling off the track and landed in a heap on the floor. "Look what you've done!" wailed Bobby as he picked up the train and reassembled it. The carriages were undamaged, but the engine had hit the side of his bed and was badly dented.

Bobby was very upset. "My brand new train is ruined!" he cried.

"Don't worry, Bobby," said his mother, "we can't take it back to the shop now, but we can take it to the toymender in the morning. I'm sure he'll make a good job of mending the engine and it'll look as good as new again." Bobby played with his racing car, he wore his new baseball cap and he read his new book, but really all he wanted to do was to play with his train set. He went to bed that night with the engine on the floor near his bed.

In the morning when Bobby woke up, the first thing he did was to look at the poor broken engine of his train set. He picked it up, expecting to see the buckled metal, but the engine was perfect. He couldn't believe his eyes! He ran to his parents. "Look, look!" he cried. They were as amazed as he was. The engine worked perfectly and Bobby played happily with his train set all day — but he made sure Freddie kept out of his room!

That night Bobby couldn't sleep. He lay in bed tossing and turning. Then he heard a noise. It was the sound of his train set rushing round the track. He peered into the darkness and yes, he could definitely make out the shape of the train as it sped by. How had the train started?

It couldn't start all by itself! Had Freddie crept into his room and flicked the switch? As his eyes gradually became accustomed to the dark Bobby could make out several shapes in the carriages. Who were the mysterious passengers? He slid out of bed and on to the floor beside the train set. Now he could see that the passengers were little folk wearing strange pointed hats and leafy costumes. "Elves!" thought Bobby.

At that moment one of the elves spotted Bobby. "Hello there!" he called as the train rushed past again. "We saw that your train set was broken. We so much wanted a ride that we fixed it. I hope you don't mind!" Bobby was too astounded to say anything at all. "Come with us for a ride," called the elf as his carriage approached again.

As the train passed him the elf leaned out of the carriage and

grabbed Bobby by the hand. Bobby felt himself shrinking as he flew through the air, and the next instant he was sitting beside the elf in the carriage of his very own train set! "Here we go — hold tight!" called the elf as the train left the track and went out through the window into the night sky.

"Now, where would you like to go? What would you like to see?" asked the elf.

"Toyland!" replied Bobby without hesitation. Sure enough, the train headed towards a track which curved up a mountain made of pink and white sugar. Beside the track were toys going about their daily business. Bobby saw a ragdoll getting into a shiny tin car. Then a wooden sailor puppet wound up the car with a large key and off went the doll. He saw three teddy bears setting off for school with their satchels on their backs. Then he saw a brightly coloured clown playing a drum.

The train stopped and Bobby and the elves got out. "Now for some fun!" said one of the elves. They had come to a halt by a toy fairground. Bobby found that this was like no other fairground he had ever been to before. For in Toyland, all the rides are real. The horses on the carousel were real horses. The dodgem cars were real cars. And when he got in the rocket for the rocket ride, it took him all the way to the moon and back!

"Time to go, Bobby," said one of the elves at last. "It'll be morning soon." Bobby climbed wearily back into the train and soon he was fast asleep. When he woke up it was morning, and he was back in his

bed. The train set lay quite still on its tracks. But in one of the carriages was a scrap of paper and on the paper, in tiny spidery writing, were the words: *We hope you enjoyed your trip to Toyland — the elves.*

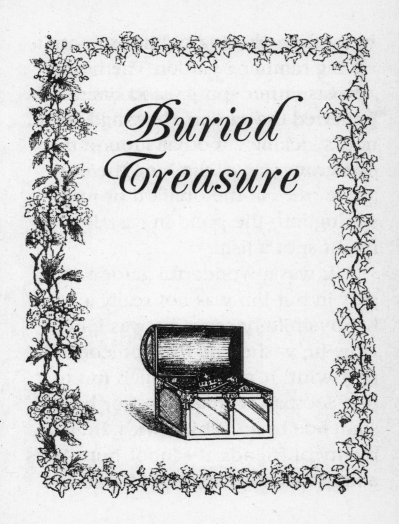

Buried Treasure

JIM LIVED in a big old house with a big rambling garden. The house was rather spooky, and Jim much preferred the garden. He would spend hours kicking a football around the overgrown lawn, climbing the old apple trees in the orchard or just staring into the pond in case he might spot a fish.

It was a wonderful garden to play in but Jim was not really a happy child because he was lonely. How he wished he had someone to play with! It would be such fun to play football with a friend, or have someone to go fishing with. He had plenty of friends at school, but it was a long bus journey to his home and besides, his school friends found his house so spooky that they only came to visit once.

One day Jim was hunting about in the garden with a stick. He hoped he might find some interesting small creatures to examine. Every time he found a new creature he would draw

it and try to find out its name. So far, he had discovered eight types of snails and six different ladybirds. As he was poking about under some leaves he saw a piece of metal sticking out of the ground. He reached down and pulled it free. In his hand lay a rusty old key. It was quite big, and as Jim brushed away the soil, he saw that it was carved with beautiful patterns.

Jim carried the key indoors and cleaned it and polished it. Then he set about trying to find the lock that it fitted. First he tried the old garden gate that had been locked as long as Jim could remember. But the key was far too small. Next he tried the grandfather clock in the hall. But the key did not fit the clock's lock. Then he remembered an old wind-up teddy bear that played the drum. Jim hadn't played with the toy for a long time and he eagerly tried out the key, but this time it was too big.

Then Jim had another idea. "Perhaps the key fits something in the attic," he thought. He was usually too scared to go into the attic on his own because it really was scary. But now he was so determined to find the key's home that he ran up the stairs boldly and opened the door. The attic was dimly lit, dusty and full of cobwebs. The water pipes hissed and creaked and Jim shivered. He

began to look under a few
dustsheets and opened some old
boxes, but didn't find anything that
looked like it needed a key to unlock
it. Then he caught sight of a large
book sticking out from one of the
shelves. It was one of those sorts of
books fitted with a lock. Jim lifted
down the book, which was
extremely heavy, and put it on the
floor. His fingers trembled as he put

the key in the lock. It fitted perfectly. He turned the key and the lock sprang open, releasing a cloud of dust. Jim wiped the dust from his eyes, slowly opened the book and turned the pages.

What a disappointment! The pages were crammed with tiny writing and there were no pictures at all. Jim was about to shut the book again when he heard a voice. The voice was coming from the book! "You have unlocked my secrets," it said. "Step into my pages if you are looking for adventure."

Jim was so curious that he found himself stepping on to the book. As soon as he put his foot on the pages he found himself falling through the book. The next thing he knew he was on the deck of a ship. He looked up and saw a tattered black flag flying from a flagpole and on the flag were a skull and cross-bones. He was on a pirate ship! He looked down and saw that he was dressed like a pirate.

The pirate ship was sailing along nicely, when suddenly Jim saw some

dangerous-looking rocks in the water — and they were heading straight for them! Before he could shout, the ship had run aground and all the pirates were jumping overboard and swimming to the shore. Jim swam, too.

The water felt deliciously warm and when he reached the shore he found warm sand between his toes. He couldn't believe it! Here he was on a desert island. The pirates went in all directions, searching for something to make a shelter. Jim looked, too, and under a rock he found a book. The book looked familiar to Jim. He was sure he'd seen it somewhere before. He was still puzzling over it when one of the pirates came running towards him waving a knife. "You thief, you stole me rubies!" cursed the pirate in a menacing voice. What was Jim to do?

Then he heard a voice call out from the book, "Quick! Step into my pages." Without thinking twice, Jim stepped into the book and suddenly he was back in the attic again.

Jim peered closely at the page from which he'd just stepped. The Pirates and the Stolen Treasure it said at the top of the page. Jim read the page and found he was reading exactly the adventure he had been in. He turned excitedly to the contents page at the front of the

book and read the chapter titles.
Journey to Mars, he read, and The
Castle Under the Sea. Further down
it said: The Magic Car and Into the
Jungle. Jim was thrilled. He realised
that he could open the book at any
page and become part of the
adventure, and he only had to find
the book and step into it to get back
to the attic again.

After that, Jim had many, many adventures. He made lots of friends in the stories and he had lots of narrow escapes. But he always found the book again just in time. Jim was never lonely again.

Catswhiskers

CATSWHISKERS was a pyjama case cat, and a very fine-looking pyjama case cat at that. Susie's granny had sewn him together when Susie was only four years old. It had taken Susie's granny quite a long time to make Catswhiskers. Every night she had sat by the fire carefully cutting and sewing, until he was perfect. Catswhiskers' body was made from the finest black velvet. He had beautiful red glass eyes, a bushy tail and the longest whiskers you have ever seen. That is how he got the name Catswhiskers.

Catswhiskers sat on the end of Susie's bed, looking at all the toys in the bedroom in that slightly snooty way that cats have of looking at things.

When Susie was asleep, or playing in another room, Catswhiskers and all the toys would talk to each other. But Catswhiskers was bored with talking to the toys. Jenny the ragdoll was — well — just a ragdoll. "What could a ragdoll possibly have to say that would be of interest to a velvet pyjama case cat?" thought Catswhiskers.

Then there was Neddy the rocking horse. He was a perfectly pleasant rocking horse as far as rocking horses went, but he only ever seemed to want to talk about how nice and shiny he was, and how he thought he was Susie's favourite toy. Even the alphabet bricks, the jack-in-the-box and the brightly coloured ball seemed to have nothing to say of interest to Cats-

whiskers. He sighed and looked at the window, wondering if life was more exciting outside.

One day, he decided he'd had enough of life in the bedroom with all the toys, and that he would venture outside to see if he could meet someone more interesting to talk to. So that night, when it was dark and Susie was asleep, he crept carefully to the open bedroom window and jumped out. It was a clear, cold, moonlit night. Catswhiskers shivered a little to find it so cold outside, and he maybe shivered a little more because he was also rather frightened. But he was very excited to be in the outside world, too, and he soon forgot about the cold and his fear.

He walked along the fence to the end of Susie's garden and jumped down into the garden next door. He had no sooner landed when he heard a fierce growl and saw two big, black eyes glinting in the moonlight.

It was Barker, next door's dog — and he didn't like cats at all. With a loud bark, Barker came rushing towards Catswhiskers. His mouth was open wide and Catswhiskers could see his big, sharp teeth. In fact, he thought that he could see all the way down into Barker's stomach! Catswhiskers only just had time to leap back on to the fence as Barker, jaws still snapping, gave chase.

"Phew, what a narrow escape," gasped Catswhiskers. "I didn't realise dogs were so unfriendly!"

He was wondering where it might be safe to go next when he heard a low, hissing voice behind him. "Hey, velvet cat," hissed the voice. "What do you think you are doing on our patch?"

Catswhiskers turned round to see the biggest, meanest-looking cat he had ever set eyes on. And behind him were several more mean-looking cats, all coming slowly towards Catswhiskers with their sharp claws at the ready. Catswhiskers didn't wait

a second longer. He simply ran for
his life. Now he was very frightened.
He was also feeling cold and hungry.
He wished that he was still in the

warm safety of Susie's bedroom with the other toys. Just as he was thinking that the outside world was perhaps a bit too exciting, he heard the sound of a van approaching. It suddenly stopped, its glaring headlights shining straight at him. On the side of the van were the words STRAY CAT CATCHER.

Out of the van stepped a man carrying a big net. Catswhiskers thought he knew just who that net was for, and decided that it was definitely time to go!

Without thinking about the dangers he might find himself in if he came face to face again with gangs of sharp-clawed cats or fierce, barking dogs, he ran back towards Susie's house as fast as his velvet legs could carry him. At last he reached the window and jumped thankfully back inside.

Snuggled down again on the warm bed with all his familiar friends around him, Catswhiskers decided that perhaps this was the best life for a pyjama case cat after all.

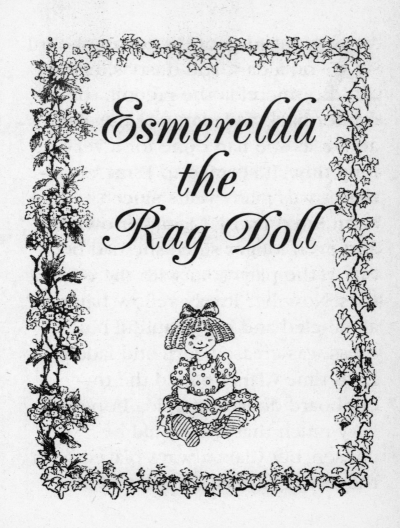

Esmerelda
the
Rag Doll

AT THE BACK of the toy cupboard on a dark and dusty shelf lay Esmerelda the ragdoll. She lay on her back and stared at the shelf above, as she had done for a very long time. It seemed to Esmerelda that it was many years since she had been lifted up by Clara, her owner, and even longer since she had been out in the playroom with the other toys. Now her lovely yellow hair was all tangled and her beautiful blue dress was creased, torn and faded. Each time Clara opened the toy cupboard door, Esmerelda hoped very much that she would be chosen, but Clara always played with the newer toys at the front of the cupboard. Every time Clara put her toys back in the cupboard, Esmerelda felt herself being pushed further towards the back. It was very uncomfortable and indeed, Esmerelda might have suffocated if it wasn't for a hole at the back of the cupboard, which enabled her to breathe.

These days Esmerelda felt very lonely. Until recently a one-eyed teddy bear had been beside her on the shelf. Then one day he had fallen through the hole at the back of the cupboard and was never seen again. Esmerelda missed him dreadfully, for he had been a lovely old teddy with a gentle nature. Now she, too, could feel herself being pushed towards the hole. She felt a mixture of excitement and fright at the prospect of falling through it. Sometimes she imagined that she would land on a soft feather bed belonging to a little girl who would really love her. At other times she

thought that the hole led to a terri-
fying land full of monsters.

One day Esmerelda heard
Clara's mother say, "Now Clara, today
you must tidy up the toy cupboard
and clear out all those old toys you
no longer play with."

Esmerelda could see Clara's
small hands reaching into the
cupboard. She couldn't bear the
thought of being picked up by the
little girl and then discarded. "There's
only one thing to do," she said to
herself. She wriggled towards the
hole, closed her eyes and jumped.
Esmerelda felt herself falling, and
then she landed with a bump on
something soft.

"Watch out, my dear!" said a familiar voice from underneath her. Esmerelda opened her eyes and saw that she had landed on One-eyed Ted.

The two toys were so overjoyed to see each other again that they hugged one another. "What shall we do now?" cried Esmerelda.

"I have an idea," said Ted. "There's a rusty old toy car over there. I wanted to escape in it, but I can't drive with only one eye. What do you think? Shall we give it a go?"

"Yes, yes!" exclaimed Esmerelda, climbing into the driver's seat.

By now One-eyed Ted had found the key and was winding up

the car. "Away we go!" he called as they sped off.

"Where are we going?" shouted Esmerelda.

"To the seaside," replied Ted.

"Which way is it?" asked Esmerelda, holding on to her yellow hair streaming behind her in the wind.

"I don't know. We'll have to ask the way," said Ted.

Rounding a bend, they came across a black cat crossing the road. "Excuse me," called Ted, "could you tell us the way to the seaside?"

Now, as you know, cats hate water. "Whatever do they want to go near water for? Why should I help them?" thought the cat. "It's the other side of that mountain," he growled as he ran off.

On sped the rusty car, and up the mountainside. When they reached the top of the mountain they met a sheep. Now, as you know, sheep never listen properly. "Excuse me," said Esmerelda, "where can we find the beach?"

Well, the silly sheep thought Esmerelda was asking where they could find a peach! "Down there," she bleated, nodding towards an orchard in the valley below.

Esmerelda and Ted leaped back into the car and sped off down the mountainside, but when they

reached the orchard there was no sign of water, of course — just a lot of peach trees.

Once again they scratched their heads in puzzlement. Just then a mole popped his head out of the earth. "Excuse me," said Ted, "would you happen to know how we can find the seaside?"

Now the mole was very wise, but unfortunately he was also, as you know, very short sighted. He peered at Esmerelda's blue dress. "That patch of blue must surely be a river, and rivers run into the sea," he thought.

"Just follow that river," he said, "and you'll end up at the seaside.

Good day!" And with that he disappeared under ground again.

Esmerelda and Ted looked even more puzzled, for there was no sign of a river in the orchard. "Oh well," sighed Esmerelda, "perhaps we'll never find the seaside."

"Don't give up," said Ted. "We'll surely find it in the end." They climbed back in the rusty car and set off again. After a short while the car started to splutter and then it came to a complete halt at the side of the

road. "What shall we do now?" cried Esmerelda.

"We'll just have to wait here and see what happens," said Ted. It seemed like a very long time that they sat beside the road. At long last they heard footsteps, and then Esmerelda felt herself being picked up.

"Look — it's a dear old tatty ragdoll," said a voice. Esmerelda looked up and saw that she was being carried by a little girl.

Ted and the rusty car had been picked up by the girl's father. "We'll take them home and look after them," the man said.

Now they were in a real car

and before long the toys found themselves in a house. The little girl carried Esmerelda, One-eyed Ted and the rusty car upstairs to her bedroom and put them down on a window sill. "I'll be back soon," she whispered.

Esmerelda looked out of the window and nearly danced for joy. "Look, look Ted," she shouted. For out of the window she could see the road, and beyond the road was a beach and then the sea. "We reached the seaside after all," she cried.

Esmerelda, Ted and the rusty car lived happily in the house beside the sea. Esmerelda's hair was brushed and plaited and she was given a beautiful new dress. Ted had a new eye sewn on and could see properly again. The rusty car was painted and oiled. Most days the little girl took her new toys down to the beach to play with, and the days in the dark toy cupboard were soon forgotten. The little girl used to tell her friends the story of how she had found her three best toys lying beside the road one day. And as for the toys, well, they sometimes talked about that strange day when they had such an adventure — and they'd burst out laughing.

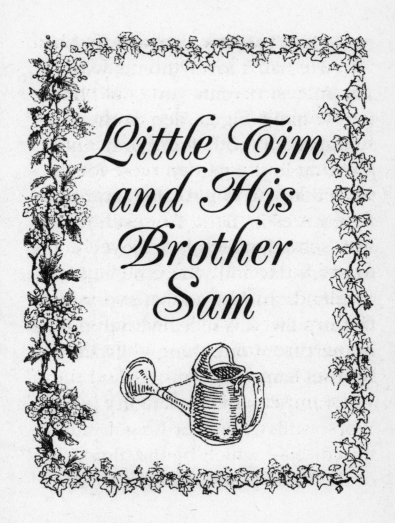

Little Tim
and His
Brother
Sam

LITTLE TIM was a very lucky boy. He had a lovely home, with the nicest parents you could hope for. He had a big garden, with a swing and a football net in it. And growing in the garden were lots of trees that you could climb and have adventures in. Little Tim even had a nice school, which he enjoyed going to every day and where he had lots of friends. In fact, almost everything in Tim's life was nice. Everything that is apart from one thing — Tim's brother Sam.

Sam was a very naughty boy. Worse still, whenever he got into mischief — which he did almost all of the time — he managed to make it look as though someone else was to blame. And that someone was usually poor Tim!

Once Sam thought that he would put salt in the sugar bowl instead of sugar. That afternoon, Sam and Tim's parents had some friends round for tea. All the guests put salt in their cups of tea, of course, thinking it was sugar. Well, being very polite they didn't like to say anything, even though their cups of tea tasted very strange indeed! When Sam and Tim's parents tasted their tea, however, they guessed immediately that someone had been playing a trick. They had to apologise to their guests and make them all fresh cups of tea. And who got the blame? Little Tim did, because Sam had sprinkled salt on Tim's bedroom floor so that their mother would think that Tim was the culprit.

Another time, Sam and Tim were playing football in the garden when Sam accidentally kicked the ball against a window and broke it. Sam immediately ran away and hid, so that when their father came out to investigate, only Tim was to be seen. So poor little Tim got the blame again.

Then there was the time when Sam and Tim's Aunt Jessica came to stay. She was a very nice lady, but she hated anything creepy-crawly, and as far as she was concerned that included frogs. So what did Sam do? Why, he went down to the garden pond and got a big, green frog to put in Aunt Jessica's handbag. When Aunt Jessica opened her handbag to get her glasses out, there staring out of the bag at her were two froggy eyes.

"Croak!" said the frog.

"Eeek!" yelled Aunt Jessica and almost jumped out of her skin.

"I told Tim not to do it," said Sam.

Tim opened his mouth and was just about to protest his innocence when his mother said, "Tim, go to your room immediately and don't come out until you are told."

Poor Tim went to his room and had to stay there until after supper. Sam thought it was very funny.

The next day, Sam decided that he would play another prank and blame it on Tim. He went to the garden shed and, one by one, took out all the garden tools. When he thought no-one was watching, he hid them all in Tim's bedroom cupboard. In went the spade, the fork, the watering can, the trowel — in fact, everything except the lawnmower. And the only reason that the lawnmower didn't go in was because it was too heavy to carry!

But this time, Sam's little prank was about to come unstuck, for Aunt

Jessica had seen him creeping up the stairs to Tim's bedroom with the garden tools. She guessed immediately what Sam was up to, and who was likely to get the blame. When Sam wasn't about, she spoke to Tim. The two of them whispered to each other for a few seconds and then smiled triumphantly.

Later that day, Sam and Tim's father went to the garden shed to do some gardening. Imagine his surprise when all he saw were some old flower pots and the lawnmower. He searched high and low for the garden tools. He looked behind the compost heap, under the garden steps, behind the sand pit and in the garage. But they weren't anywhere to be seen.

Then he started searching in the house. He looked in the kitchen cupboard, and was just looking under the stairs when something at the top of the stairs caught his eye. The handle from the garden spade was sticking out of the door to Sam's bedroom. Looking rather puzzled, he went upstairs and walked into Sam's bedroom. There, nestling neatly in the cupboard, were the rest of the tools.

"Sam, come up here immediately," called his father.

Sam, not realising anything was amiss, came sauntering upstairs. Suddenly he saw all the garden tools that he had so carefully hidden in Tim's cupboard now sitting in his cupboard. He was speechless.

"Right," said his father, "before you go out to play, you can take all the tools back down to the garden shed. Then you can cut the grass. Then you can dig over the flower beds, and then you can do the weeding."

Well, it took Sam hours to do all the gardening. Tim and Aunt Jessica watched from the window and clutched their sides with laughter. Sam never did find out how all the garden tools found their way into his bedroom, but I think you've guessed, haven't you?

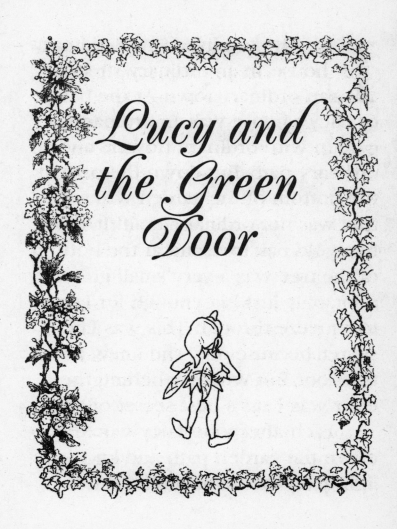

Lucy and the Green Door

LUCY JENKINS lived in an ordinary house, in an ordinary street, in an ordinary town. At the back of Lucy's house was an ordinary garden with ordinary flowers and an ordinary path. But down the path at the bottom of the garden was a tree that was not ordinary at all! It was a huge old oak tree, and at the bottom of the tree was a very small green door, only just big enough for Lucy to squeeze through. This was Lucy's secret, because only she knew about the door. But what lay behind the door was Lucy's best secret of all!

Each afternoon Lucy would go down the garden path and knock lightly on the door. On the third knock the door would swing open wide, and the chief elf would be there to welcome her inside.

"Come inside, little Lucy," the elf would always say, "and have some tea."

Inside, Lucy would meet some very special friends indeed! First there were Penelope and Geraldine, two of the gentlest and sweetest fairies it was possible to imagine. Then there were Basil and Granville, who were rather mischievous imps (but who made Lucy laugh with their tricks and jokes), and there were the storytellers, who would sit for hours with Lucy and tell her the greatest tales from all the corners of the world. And of course there was the chief elf, who would make the most delicious milkshakes and scones with heaps of cream for Lucy to eat.

The world behind the green door was a wonderful place, and Lucy would always go home after-

wards feeling very cheerful and jolly. On one particular visit to the world behind the green door Lucy had just finished a scrumptious tea of cocoa and toasted marshmallows with the chief elf, when she went off to play games with Basil and Granville. They were playing blind man's buff, and Lucy roared with laughter as Basil sneaked up on the blindfolded Granville and tickled him in the ribs, making him squeal and beg for the teasing to stop.

Now just recently, Lucy had been feeling down in the dumps because very soon she would be going to school and would only be able to visit her friends at weekends.

But they assured her that they would never forget her, and that as long as she was always a true friend to them she could visit as often or as little as she liked. This cheered Lucy up considerably, and then they took her to visit the storytellers so that her happiness was complete. Of all the delights behind the green door, the storytellers were Lucy's favourite. They told her stories of how the whales had learned to sing, and of where the stars went when the sun had risen in the sky and they had slipped from view.

Because of the assurances of the fairies, Lucy was not too worried when the day finally came for her to join all the other boys and girls of her age at school. Every day, Lucy would go to school and then afterwards would visit her friends behind the green door. As winter came round and the days grew dark she only visited at weekends, and looked forward to the holidays when she could visit them every day once more.

Meanwhile, at school, Lucy had made friends with a girl called Jessica, and although she told Jessica

all about her family and her home, she didn't at first tell her about her extraordinary tree with the little green door and the magic world that lay beyond. Lucy did tell Jessica all the stories that she was told by the storytellers, however, and Jessica grew more and more curious about

where she had heard all the wonderful tales. Every day, Jessica would ask more and more questions, and Lucy found it more and more difficult to avoid telling her about her secret. Eventually, Lucy gave in and told Jessica all about her adventures behind the green door.

Jessica scoffed and laughed when Lucy told her about the chief elf, and Basil, Granville, Penelope and Geraldine. She howled with laughter at the thought of the wonderful teas and the stories that followed. Jessica thought that Lucy was making the whole thing up! When Lucy protested, and said it was true, Jessica told her that it simply wasn't possible — that there were no such things as elves and fairies and imps and strange and wonderful worlds behind doors in trees. Lucy was distraught, and decided to take Jessica to the green door.

On the way home Lucy started to worry. What if she really had imagined it all? But if her wonderful friends didn't exist, how could she possibly know them? Jessica walked beside Lucy, still teasing her and laughing about Lucy's 'invisible' friends!

When Lucy and Jessica reached the bottom of the garden, Lucy was about to tap lightly on the green door at the bottom of the oak tree when she suddenly noticed the door had disappeared. She rubbed her eyes and looked again, but it simply wasn't there!

Jessica smirked and laughed at Lucy, calling her silly and babyish to believe in magic and fairy tales, and then ran off back down the road to school. Lucy could not face going back to school that afternoon, and when her mother saw her enter the house she thought she must be ill — she looked so upset! Lucy went to bed early and cried herself to sleep.

And when Lucy slept she started to dream. The chief elf, Basil and Granville, Penelope and Geraldine and the storytellers were all there in the dream.

Then Penelope and Geraldine stepped forward and hugged Lucy, and the hug was so real that Lucy began to hope it wasn't a dream! Then they all hugged her and asked why she hadn't been to see them for so long, and why they had not been able to reach out to her except now in the deepest of sleeps. Lucy explained what had happened on her last visit, and told them all about Jessica, and then Geraldine spoke.

"Little Lucy," she said, "you are special. You believe in magic and you believe in the little people. And because you believe, you are able to see us and live among us. But those who don't believe will always be shut out from our world. You must keep your belief, little Lucy."

With a huge surge of happiness

Lucy woke up, dressed quickly and ran out of her ordinary house, down the ordinary path in the ordinary garden up to the extraordinary tree, and was delighted to see the green door once more! She knocked very lightly and, after the third tap, the door swung open to reveal the chief elf. "Come inside, little Lucy," the elf said happily, "and have some tea."

Rusty's Big Day

LONG AGO there lived a poor farmer called Fred, who had a horse called Rusty. Once Rusty had been a good, strong horse. He had willingly pulled the plough and taken his master into town to sell his vegetables. Now he was too old to work on the farm, but the farmer couldn't bear to think of getting rid of him because he was so sweet-natured. "It would be like turning away one of my own family," Fred used to say. Rusty spent his days grazing in the corner of the field. He was quite content, but he felt sad that he was no longer able to help the poor farmer earn his living.

One day, Fred decided to go to

town to sell a few vegetables. He
harnessed Beauty, the young mare, to
the wagon and off they went. Beauty
shook her fine mane and tossed a
glance at Rusty as if to say, "Look
who's queen of the farmyard!"

While Fred was in the town, his
eye was caught by a notice pinned
to a tree. It said:

HORSE PARADE
at 2 pm today

The winner will pull the King's carriage to the Grand Banquet tonight

"There's not a moment to lose, my girl!" said Fred. "We must get you ready for the parade." So saying, he turned the wagon around. "Giddy-up, Beauty!" he called, and she trotted all the way back to the farm.

Fred set to work to make Beauty look more lovely than she had ever done before. He scrubbed her hoofs and brushed her coat until it shone. Then he plaited her mane and tied it with a bright red ribbon. Rusty watched from the field. "How fine she looks," he thought, wistfully. "She's sure to win." He felt a bit sad that he was too old to take part in the parade, so he found a patch of the sweetest grass to graze on, to console himself.

All at once, he heard Fred approach. "Come on, old boy," he said, "you can come, too. It'll be fun for you to watch the parade, won't it?" Rusty was thrilled. It seemed such a long time since the master had last taken him into town. Fred brushed Rusty's coat, too. "You want to look your best, don't you now, old boy?" he said.

Soon the three of them set off back into town, with Fred riding on Beauty's back and Rusty walking by their side. When they reached the parade ground, there were already a lot of horses gathered there with their owners. There were horses of every shape and size — small, skinny ones, big, muscular ones and there were even big, skinny ones, too!

Soon it was time for the parade to begin. The king entered the parade ground, followed by the members of the royal court. They took their places at one end of the ground. Then the king announced three contests. First there would be a race. The horses would gallop from one end of the parade ground to the other. Then there would be a contest of strength. Each horse would have to try and pull a heavy carriage. Lastly, there would be a trotting competition. Each horse would have to carry a rider around the parade ground.

The competition began. All the horses lined up at the starting line. "Come on, Rusty. Have a go!" whispered Fred. He led Rusty and Beauty to where the other horses were lined up.

All the other horses turned and

stared. "What's an old horse like you doing taking part in a contest like this?" one of them asked disdainfully.

"You won't make it past the starting line!" taunted another.

Rusty said nothing and took his place at the start. Then they were off down the field. Rusty felt his heart pounding and his feet fly like never before, but try as he might he just couldn't keep up with the others and came in last.

"What did you expect?" snorted the other horses turning their backs on poor old Rusty.

However, Rusty was not down-cast "Speed isn't everything," he said to himself.

Now it was time for the test of strength. One by one the horses took it in turns to pull the carriage. When it was Rusty's turn, he tried his best. He felt every muscle in his aching body strain, as he slowly pulled the carriage along.

"Not a hope!" declared the other horses.

"Strength isn't everything," said Rusty to himself.

Next it was time for the trotting competition. "I shall ride each horse in turn," declared the king. He climbed up on to the first horse, but it bolted away so fast that the king was left hanging by the stirrups. The next horse lifted his legs so high that he threw the king right up in the air and he might have hurt himself badly, if he hadn't been caught by one of his courtiers. The next horse was so nervous about carrying the king that his teeth chattered, and the king had to put his fingers in his ears. Then it was Beauty's turn and she carried the king magnificently, until she stumbled at the end. At last it was Rusty's turn. The other horses sniggered, "Let's see that old horse make a fool of himself!"

Rusty carried the king quite slowly and steadily, making sure he picked his feet up carefully, so that his royal highness would not be jolted.

"Thank you for a most pleasant ride," said the king dismounting. There was a hush as the horses and their owners awaited the result of the contest.

"I have decided," announced the king, "that Rusty is the winner. Not only did he give me a most comfortable ride, but he accepted his other defeats with dignity. Speed and strength are not everything, you know."

Rusty and Fred were overjoyed, and even Beauty offered her congratulations. "Though I might have won if I hadn't stumbled," she muttered.

So Rusty proudly pulled the king's carriage that evening, and he made such a good job of it that the king asked him if he would do it again the following year. Then the king asked Fred if his daughter could ride Beauty from time to time. He even gave Fred a bag of gold to pay for the horses' upkeep. So the three of them were happy as they never had been before as they returned home to the farm that night.

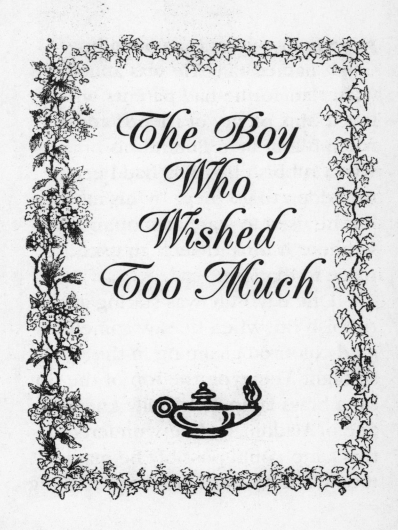

The Boy Who Wished Too Much

THERE ONCE WAS a young boy named Billy. He was a lucky lad, for he had parents who loved him, plenty of friends and a room full of toys. Behind his house was a rubbish tip. Billy had been forbidden to go there by his mother, but he used to stare at it out of the window. It looked such an exciting place to explore.

One day, Billy was staring at the rubbish tip, when he saw something gold-coloured gleaming in the sunlight. There, on the top of the tip, sat a brass lamp. Now Billy knew the tale of Aladdin, and he wondered if this lamp could possibly be magic, too. When his mother wasn't looking he slipped out of the back door, scrambled up the tip and snatched the lamp from the top.

Billy ran to the garden shed. It was quite dark inside, but Billy could see the brass of the lamp glowing softly in his hands. When his eyes had grown accustomed to the dark, he saw that the lamp was quite dirty. As he started to rub at the brass, there was a puff of smoke and the

shed was filled with light. Billy closed his eyes tightly and when he opened them again, he found to his astonishment that there was a man standing there, dressed in a costume richly embroidered with gold and jewels. "I am the genie of the lamp," he said. "Are you by any chance Aladdin?"

"N… n… no, I'm Billy," stammered Billy, staring in disbelief.

"How very confusing," said the genie frowning. "I was told that the boy with the lamp was named Aladdin. Oh well, never mind! Now I'm here, I may as well grant you your wishes. You can have three, by the way."

At first Billy was so astonished he couldn't speak. Then he began to think hard. What would be the very best thing to wish for? He had an idea. "My first wish," he said, "is that I can have as many wishes as I want."

The genie looked rather taken aback, but then he smiled and said, "A wish is a wish. So be it!"

Billy could hardly believe his ears. Was he really going to get all his wishes granted? He decided to start with a really big wish, just in case the genie changed his mind later. "I wish I could have a purse that never runs out of money," he said.

Hey presto! There in his hand was a purse with five coins in it.

Without remembering to thank the genie, Billy ran out of the shed and down the road to the sweet shop. He bought a large bag of sweets and took one of the coins out of his purse to pay for it. Then he peeped cautiously inside the purse, and

sure enough there were still five coins.

The magic had worked! Billy ran back to the garden shed to get his next wish, but the genie had vanished. "That's not fair!" cried Billy, stamping his foot. Then he remembered the lamp. He seized it and rubbed at it furiously. Sure enough, the genie reappeared.

"Don't forget to share those sweets with your friends," he said. "What is your wish, Billy?"

This time Billy, who was very fond of sweet things, said, "I wish I had a house made of chocolate!"

No sooner had he uttered the words than he found that he was

standing outside a house made
entirely of rich, creamy chocolate.
Billy broke off the door knocker and
nibbled at it. Yes, it really was made
of the most delicious chocolate that
he had ever tasted! Billy gorged
himself until he began to feel quite
sick. He lay down on the grass and
closed his eyes. When he opened
them again, the chocolate house had
vanished and he was outside the
garden shed once more. "It's not fair
to take my chocolate house away. I
want it back!" he complained,
stamping his foot once again.

Billy went back into the shed.
"This time I'll ask for something that
lasts longer," he thought. He rubbed

the lamp and there stood the genie again.

"You've got chocolate all around your mouth," said the genie disapprovingly. "What is your wish?"

"I wish I had a magic carpet to take me to faraway lands," said Billy. No sooner were the words out of his mouth than he could feel himself being lifted up and out of the shed on a lovely soft carpet. The carpet took Billy up, up and away over hills, mountains and seas to the end of the Earth. He saw camels in the desert, polar bears at the North Pole and whales far out at sea. At last, Billy began to feel homesick and he asked the magic carpet to take him home.

Soon he was back in his own garden again.

Billy was beginning to feel very powerful and important. He began to wish for more and more things. He wished that he did not have to go to school — and so he didn't! He wished that he had a servant to clear up after him and a cook to make him special meals of sweet things — and a cook and a servant appeared.

Billy began to get very fat and lazy. His parents despaired at how spoiled he had become. His friends no longer came to play because he had grown so boastful.

One morning, Billy woke up, looked in the mirror and burst into tears. "I'm so lonely and unhappy!" he wailed. He realised that there was only one thing to do. He ran down to the garden shed, picked up the lamp and rubbed it.

"You don't look very happy," said the genie, giving him a concerned glance. "What is your wish?"

"I wish everything was back to normal," Billy blurted out, "and I wish I could have no more wishes!"

"A wise choice!" said the genie. "So be it. Goodbye, Billy!" And with that the genie vanished. Billy stepped out of the shed, and from then on everything was normal again. His parents cared for him, he went to school and his friends came to play once more. But Billy had learned his lesson. He never boasted again and he always shared his sweets and toys.

The Castle in the Clouds

THERE WAS ONCE a family that lived in a little house in a village at the bottom of a mountain. At the top of the mountain was a great, grey castle made of granite. The castle was always shrouded in clouds, so it was known as the castle in the clouds. From the village you could only just see the outline of its high walls and turrets. No-one in the village ever went near the castle, for it looked such a gloomy and forbidding place.

Now in this family there were seven children. One by one they went out into the world to seek their fortune, and at last it was the youngest child's turn. His name was

Sam. His only possession was a pet cat named Jess, and she was an excellent rat-catcher. Sam was most upset at the thought of leaving Jess behind when he went off to find work, but then he had an idea.

"I'll offer Jess's services at the castle in the clouds. They're bound

to need a good ratter, and I'm sure I can find work there, too," he thought.

His parents were dismayed to discover that Sam intended to seek work at the castle, but try as they might they could not change his mind. So Sam set off for the castle with Jess at his side. Soon the road started to wind up the mountainside through thick pine forests. It grew cold and misty. Rounding a bend they suddenly found themselves up against a massive, grey stone wall. They followed the curve of the wall until they came to the castle door.

Sam went up to the door and banged on it. The sound echoed

spookily. "Who goes there?" said a voice.

Looking up, Sam saw that a window high in the wall had been thrown open and a face was eyeing him suspiciously. "I… I… I wondered if you'd be interested in employing my cat as a rat-catcher," began Sam.

The window slammed shut, but a moment later a hand beckoned him through the partly open castle door. Stepping inside, Sam and Jess found themselves face-to-face with an old man.

"Rat-catcher, did you say?" said the old man raising one eyebrow. "Very well, but she'd better do a good job or my master will punish us all!"

Sam sent Jess off to prove her worth. In the meantime Sam asked the old man, who was the castle guard, if there might be any work for him, too.

"You can help out in the kitchens. It's hard work, mind!" the guard said.

Sam was soon at work in the kitchens — and what hard work it was! He spent all day peeling vegetables, cleaning pans and scrubbing the floor. By midnight he was exhausted. He was about to find a patch of straw to make his bed, when he noticed Jess wasn't around. He set off in search of her. Down

dark passages he went, up winding staircases, looking in every corner and behind every door, but there was no sign of her. By now he was hopelessly lost and was wondering how he would ever find his way back to the kitchens, when he caught sight of Jess's green eyes shining like lanterns at the top of a rickety spiral staircase. "Here, Jess!" called Sam softly. But Jess stayed just where she was.

When he reached her, he found that she was sitting outside a door and seemed to be listening to something on the other side. Sam put his ear to the door. He could hear the sound of sobbing. He knocked gently at the door. "Who is it?" said a girl's voice.

"I'm Sam, the kitchen boy. What's the matter? Can I come in?" said Sam.

"If only you could," sobbed the voice. "I'm Princess Rose. When my father died my uncle locked me in here so that he could steal the castle. Now I fear I shall never escape!"

Sam pushed and pushed at the door, but to no avail. "Don't worry," he said, "I'll get you out of here."

Sam knew exactly what to do, for when he had been talking to the guard, he had spotted a pair of keys hanging on a nail in the rafters high above the old man's head. He had wondered at the time why anyone should put keys out of the reach of any human hand. Now he thought he knew — but first he had to get the keys himself!

Sam and Jess finally made their way back to where the keys were, only to find the guard was fast asleep in his chair right underneath them! Quick as a flash, Jess had leaped up on to the shelf behind his head. From there, she climbed higher and higher until she reached the rafters. She took the keys in her jaws and carried them gingerly down. But as she jumped from the shelf again, she knocked over a jug and sent it crashing to the floor. The guard woke with a start.

"Who goes there?" he growled. He just caught sight of the tip of

Jess's tail as she made a dash for the door.

Sam and Jess retraced their steps with the guard in hot pursuit.

"You go a different way," hissed Sam, running up the stairs to Rose's door, while the old man disappeared off after Jess. Sam put one of the keys in the lock. It fitted! He turned the key and opened the door. There stood the loveliest girl he had ever seen. The princess ran towards him, as he cried, "Quick! There's not a moment to lose." He grabbed her hand and led her out of the tower.

"Give me the keys," she said. She led him down to the castle cellars. At last they came to a tiny door. The princess put the second key in the lock and the door opened. Inside was a small cupboard, and inside that was a golden casket filled with precious jewels.

"My own casket — stolen by my uncle," cried Rose.

Grabbing the casket the pair ran

to the stables and saddled a horse.
Suddenly Jess appeared with the
guard still chasing him. With a mighty
leap Jess landed on the back of the
horse behind the princess and Sam.

"Off we go!" cried Sam.

And that was the last that any of
them saw of the castle in the clouds.
Sam married the princess and they
all lived happily ever after.

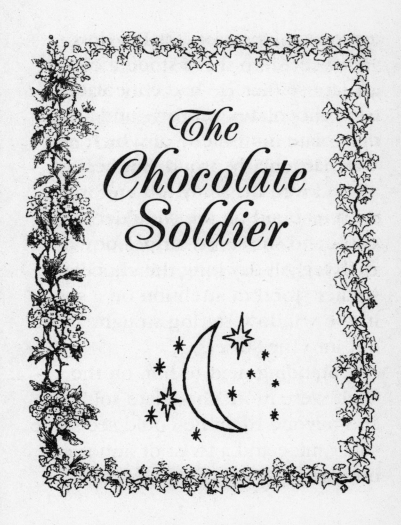

The Chocolate Soldier

IN THE WINDOW of Mrs Brown's sweet shop there stood a chocolate soldier. He had chocolate ears, chocolate eyebrows and a curly chocolate moustache of which he was particularly proud. But best of all he loved his shiny foil uniform with its braid on the shoulders and cuffs, and smart red stripes down each leg. All day long the chocolate soldier stood to attention on a shelf in the window, staring straight ahead out into the street.

Standing next to him on the shelf were more chocolate soldiers, and beyond them he could see some sugar mice and a twist of liquorice bootlaces.

It was summer time and the sun shone through the window of the sweet shop. At first the chocolate soldier felt pleasantly warm; then he started to feel uncomfortably hot. Next he began to feel most peculiar indeed. His chocolate moustache was wilting and his arms were dripping. Soon he was completely melted and before he knew it, he had slipped out through a hole in his silver foil shoe and was pouring off the shelf and out into the street.

Down the street he poured.

"Stop! Help!" he shouted, but nobody heard his cries. Now he could hear the sound of gushing water and, to his horror, he could see he was heading for a stream at the bottom of the street.

"Help me! I can't swim! I'm going to drown!" the chocolate soldier cried as he plunged into the cold, running water. But now something very strange was happening. He found he could swim quite easily. He looked round and saw that he had a chocolate tail covered in scales. He looked down at his arms, but there was a pair of fins instead. The cold water had hardened him into the shape of a chocolate fish!

The chocolate soldier was carried downstream, and after a while the stream broadened out and became a river. He realised that he would soon be carried out to sea.

"Whatever shall I do?" wondered the chocolate soldier. "I'm sure to get eaten by a bigger fish or maybe even a shark!" He tried to turn around and swim against the river's flow but it was no good. The current swept him away down river again.

Soon he could see the waves on the shore. He smelt the sea air and tasted the salt in the water. Now he found himself bobbing up and down on the sea. He could see a boat not far away and then all of a sudden he felt a net closing around him. He struggled to get out, but the net only tightened and soon he felt himself being hauled out of the water and landed with a "thwack!" on the deck among a pile of fish. The smell was awful, and the chocolate soldier was quite relieved when he felt the boat being rowed towards the shore.

"I'll hop over the side as soon as we land and run away," he thought, quite forgetting that he had no legs but only a fish's tail.

But there was no chance of escape. As soon as the boat reached the shore, he and all the other fish were flung into buckets and lifted into a van. The van stopped outside a shop and a man carried the buckets inside, where it smelt of fried fish, chips and vinegar. The chocolate soldier found himself being lifted up with a lot of other fish in a huge metal basket. He looked down and saw a terrible sight below. They were heading for a vat of boiling oil! At that very moment he felt very peculiar once again. His scales melted, his tail drooped and he felt himself slide through the holes in the basket and into the pocket of a man's overalls.

The chocolate soldier lay in the corner of the pocket, while the man worked all day in the shop. Then the man headed for home, with the chocolate soldier bouncing up and down in the overall pocket as the man walked along. Soon they arrived at the man's house. He reached into his pocket.

"Look what I've found," he said to his small son. "A coin. Here, you can have it — but don't spend it all at once!" he said, chuckling to himself. The chocolate soldier felt himself being passed from one hand to another.

"So now I've hardened into the

shape of a chocolate coin," he thought. "And I'm going to be eaten by the boy!" But to his surprise he found himself being slipped into the boy's pocket.

The chocolate soldier felt himself bouncing up and down in the child's pocket as he ran up the street and into a shop. The chocolate soldier peeped out and to his astonishment saw that he was back in Mrs Brown's sweet shop. Then he realised what was happening. The boy believed he was a real coin and was going to try and spend him! The boy stood in the queue at the counter.

The chocolate soldier called out

to his soldier friends in the window, "Pssst! It's me! Help me get out of here!" One of the soldiers looked down, but all he could see was a chocolate coin sticking out of the boy's pocket. Then he recognised the voice.

"I'm a chocolate soldier like you, but I've been turned into a coin. Help!" cried the chocolate soldier.

"Leave it to me," replied the soldier on the shelf. "Don't worry, we'll have you out of there in a jiffy!"

The word was passed along and, quick as a flash, one of the sugar mice chewed off a length of liquorice bootlace. Then the soldier lowered the lace into the boy's pocket, where it stuck to the chocolate coin. Carefully the soldiers hauled the coin up on to the shelf. The chocolate soldier was delighted to find his foil uniform was still there on the shelf, just where it had been before. All the effort of getting on to the shelf had made him quite warm, and he found he could slip quite easily back through the hole in the shoe and into his uniform again.

"I'd like a chocolate soldier," said the boy to Mrs Brown. But when he reached in his pocket the coin had gone.

"Never mind," said kind Mrs Brown, "I'll let you have one anyway."

She reached into the window and took down a soldier from the end of the row and gave it to the boy. And as for our chocolate soldier? In the cool of the night he turned back into a smart-looking soldier again.

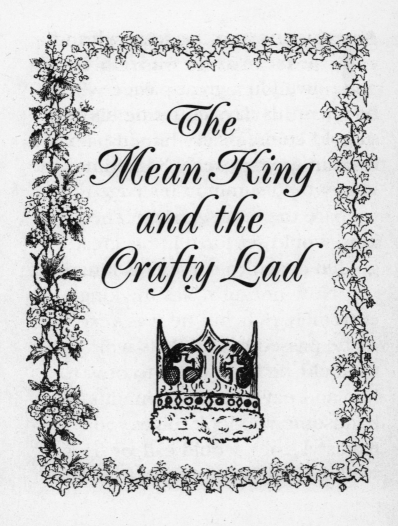

The Mean King and the Crafty Lad

THERE WAS ONCE a king who was as mean as he was rich. He lived in a great palace where he spent his days counting his bags of gold coins. Meanwhile his subjects lived in great poverty. Sometimes the king would summon his page to prepare the royal carriage. Then the king would set forth in his great, golden coach to survey his kingdom.

Now not only was the king extremely rich, but he was very vain. As he passed his subjects working in the field, he liked them to bow to him and pay him compliments. "How handsome you look today, your majesty!" they would call, or "How well the colour pink suits you, Sire!"

His head would swell with pride as he moved on. "My people truly adore me!" he would say.

But for all their complimentary words, the people hated their king. They resented the fact that the king lived in splendour while his subjects toiled hard all their lives. At last a secret meeting was called among the peasants.

"Let's sign a petition demanding our rights!" cried one man.

"And fair pay!" shouted another. They all cheered and clapped their hands.

"Who's going to write down our demands?" called an old woman. Now the crowd was hushed, for none of them knew how to read or write.

"I know what we can do instead," called a voice from the back. Everyone turned round to see a young lad in rags. "Let's march on the palace!" he cried.

"Yes!" roared the crowd.

As the angry mob reached the palace, the king saw them and sent out his guard dogs. The peasants were forced to flee for their lives with the dogs snapping at their ankles. Not until the last peasant was out of sight did the king call off his dogs. "Good work!" he cried.

From then on, however, life became even harder for the people because the king was on his guard in case they marched on the castle again. Now, when he went out and about in his kingdom, he was always accompanied by his hounds.

Eventually, another secret meeting was called. "What can we do?" the people said. "We will never be able to get past those savage dogs."

"I've got an idea," came a familiar voice. It was the ragged lad again. For a while there was uproar as folk accused him of having nearly lost them their lives. "Please trust me," pleaded the lad. "I know I let you down, but this time I've got a well thought-out plan to get the king to give up his money." In the end, the peasants listened to the boy's scheme and decided to let him try.

The next day, the boy hid in a branch of a tree that overhung the palace garden. With him he had some dog biscuits, in which he had hidden a powerful sleeping pill. He threw the biscuits on o the palace lawn and waited.

Some time later, as the boy had hoped, the king's hounds came out on to the lawn. They headed straight for the biscuits and gobbled them up. Soon they were fast asleep, one and all.

Quickly the lad slid out of the tree and, donning a large black cape, he ran round to the front of the palace and rapped on the door. A sentry opened the door. "Good day," said the lad, "I am Victor, the world-famous vet. Do you have any animals requiring medical attention?"

"No," replied the sentry, slamming the door in the lad's face. Just then voices could be heard from within the palace.

After a few moments, the sentry opened the door again and said, "As a matter of fact, we do have a bit of a problem. Step inside."

The sentry led the lad out to the lawn where the king was weeping over the dogs' bodies.

"Oh, please help," he cried. "I need my dogs. Without them I may be besieged by my own people."

The lad pretended to examine the dogs. He said to the king, "I have only seen one case like this before. The only cure is to feed the animals liquid gold."

"Liquid gold?" exclaimed the king. "Wherever shall I find liquid gold?"

"Fear not," said the lad, "I have a friend — a witch — who lives in the mountains. She can turn gold coins into liquid gold. You must let me take the dogs — and a bag of gold — to her and she will cure them."

Well, the king was so beside himself with fear that he readily agreed. The sleeping dogs were loaded on to a horse-drawn cart, and the king gave the lad a bag of gold saying, "Hurry back, my dogs are most precious."

Off went the lad, back to his home. His mother and father helped him unload the dogs, who by now were beginning to wake up. They took great care of the dogs, who

were glad to be looked after kindly for once. The next day the lad put on the cloak again and returned to the palace.

"The good news is," he said to the king, "that the cure is working. The bad news is that there was only enough gold to revive one dog. I'll need all the gold you've got to cure the others."

"Take it all," screamed the king, "only I must have my dogs back tomorrow!" He opened the safe and threw his entire stock of gold on to another cart, which the young lad dragged away.

That night the lad gave each of the king's subjects a bag of gold. The next morning he led the dogs back to the palace. To his surprise, the king didn't want them back.

"Now I have no gold," he said, "I don't need guard dogs."

Then the lad saw that the king had learned his lesson, and he told the king what had really happened.

And to everyone's joy, the king said the peasants could keep their bags of gold. As for the king, he kept the dogs as pets and became a much nicer person.

The Missing Scarf

KANGA WAS VERY proud of her stripy knitted scarf. She had made it herself and she had also made a smaller matching one for her son, Joey. Kanga used to hop through the bush with her scarf streaming out behind her, while Joey's could just be seen poking out of the top of her pouch. Now Joey was older, he was too big for Kanga's pouch, but he still wore his scarf as he hopped along beside his mother.

Then one day Kanga woke up to

find that her beautiful scarf was missing. She searched high and low but it was nowhere to be found. Eventually she decided that she would have to go out into the bush to look for it.

"Stay here," she said to Joey. "I'll try not to be long. I'm sure to find my scarf soon." Kanga hopped off into the bush and started to search among the roots of trees and under stones.

She had gone quite a long way when, looking up into the branches of a eucalyptus tree, she spotted Koala. Now Koala was usually to be found asleep, but this time she was busy preparing a meal of eucalyptus leaves for her children. Kanga looked up at Koala and then her jaw dropped. For Koala was quite clearly wearing Kanga's scarf around her tummy. Then, to Kanga's horror, she saw Koala use the end of the scarf to wipe the teacups! "Koala," Kanga called. "Whatever do you think you're doing?"

Koala stopped cleaning the teacups and looked down through the branches of the eucalyptus tree at Kanga. "I'm wiping my teacups with my apron," she replied sleepily, "and I'll thank you not to interfere!" And with that, she yawned and moved several branches further up the tree.

Poor Kanga felt very embarrassed. How could she have mistaken Koala's striped apron for her own scarf? She hopped away and carried on further into the bush. After a while she could hear Kookaburra's familiar laughing call nearby.

"I know," thought Kanga, "I'll ask her if she's seen my scarf. She'd be able to spot it easily from up in the sky." She followed the sound of Kookaburra's call until she came to the tree where she lived. She looked up and, sure enough, there was Kookaburra flying towards the tree. Kanga was about to call up when her jaw dropped again. For Kookaburra was quite clearly carrying

Kanga's scarf in her beak. "Kooka-burra," Kanga called. "Whatever do you think you're doing?"

"I'm lining my nest," mumbled Kookaburra through a beakful of stripy feathers. "And I'll thank you not to interfere," she added more distinctly, for she had now reached the nest and was arranging the feathers carefully in place.

Poor Kanga felt even more embarrassed. How could she have mistaken the feathers for her own scarf? She hopped away and carried on further into the bush.

After a while she reached a wide open plain and there she saw Emu running past with his baby chicks on his back. As he rushed past, Kanga's jaw dropped yet again. For Emu quite clearly had Kanga's scarf tucked in among his chicks. "Emu," called Kanga. "Whatever do you think you're doing?"

"I'm taking my chicks to safety," said Emu, glancing up at the sky as he sped away. "And you'd be wise to do the same," he added. Then Kanga

realised that what she had thought was her rolled-up scarf were just the striped chicks on Emu's back.

Poor Kanga felt even more embarrassed. How could she have made such a mistake? Then she felt a few spots of rain on her nose and, looking up, saw a huge black cloud overhead. There was no time to lose — she must find shelter.

She made a dash for some trees at the edge of the plain and soon found herself by a stream. She wandered along beside the stream feeling cold, wet, tired and miserable. Finally, she lay down in the wet grass beside the stream and tried to get to sleep. She shivered with cold and wondered how Joey was and whether he was behaving himself. She so hoped he hadn't got into mischief.

Just then there was a tap on her shoulder and there stood Platypus. "I could hear you in my burrow over there," she said pointing towards a hole beside the stream just above the water. "I thought you might like this to keep you warm," she added.

"My scarf!" exclaimed Kanga.

"Oh, is that what it is? I'm ever so sorry," said Platypus. "I've been using it as a blanket for my babies. It's rather cold and damp in my burrow, you know," she added, rather forlornly.

"Where did you find it?" asked Kanga.

"It was stuck on some thorns and I know I shouldn't have taken it, but I just thought it would be so nice for keeping my young ones warm," blurted Platypus, and she started to sob.

"There now," said Kanga, "don't cry. You can keep the scarf. You need it more than me."

Platypus stopped crying and

looked overjoyed. "Thank you," she said.

"No, thank you," said Kanga. "I've learned a lesson, which is not to get upset over a scarf, for I've ended up falling out with my friends."

Kanga made her way back home, but it took a long time because she apologised to all her friends on the way. When she explained what had happened Emu, Kookaburra and Koala all forgave her, and by the time she reached home she was feeling much better. Joey was there to greet her. "What have you been up to while I was away?" she asked.

"I made you this," he said. He

handed her a scarf. It was a very funny-looking scarf, made out of twigs, grass and feathers, but Kanga loved it very much.

"This is much more special than my old scarf," she said. And she gave Joey an extra big hug.

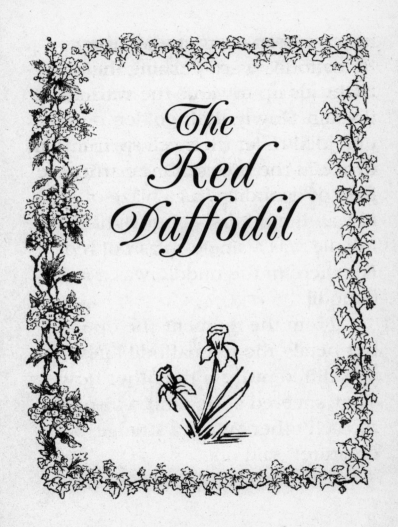

The Red Daffodil

IT WAS SPRING TIME and all the daffodils were pushing their heads up towards the warmth of the sun. Slowly, their golden petals unfolded to let their yellow trumpets dance in the breeze. One particular field of daffodils was a blaze of gold like all the others — but right in the middle was a single splash of red. For there in the middle was a red daffodil.

From the moment she opened her petals, the red daffodil knew she was different from the other flowers. They sneered at her and whispered to each other. "What a strange, poor creature!" said one.

"She must envy our beautiful

golden colour," said another.

And indeed it was true. The red daffodil wished very much that she was like the others. Instead of being proud of her red petals, she was ashamed and hung her head low. "What's wrong with me?" she thought. "Why aren't there any other red daffodils in the field?"

Passers-by stopped to admire the field of beautiful daffodils. "What a wonderful sight!" they exclaimed. And the daffodils' heads swelled with pride and danced in the breeze all the more merrily.

Then someone spotted the red daffodil right in the middle of the field. "Look at that extraordinary flower!" the man shouted. Everyone peered into the centre of the field.

"You're right," said someone else, "there's a red daffodil in the middle." Soon a large crowd had gathered, all pointing and laughing at the red daffodil.

She could feel herself blushing even redder at the attention. "How I wish my petals would close up again," she said to herself in anguish. But try as she might, her fine red trumpet stood out for all to see.

Now, in the crowd of people gathered at the edge of the field was a little girl. People were pushing and shoving and she couldn't see anything at all. At last, her father lifted her high upon his shoulders so that she could see into the field.

"Oh!" exclaimed the little girl in

a very big voice. "So that's the red daffodil. I think it's really beautiful. What a lucky daffodil to be so different."

And do you know, other people heard what the little girl said and they began to whisper to each other, "Well, I must say, I actually thought myself it was rather pretty, you know." Before long, people were praising the daffodil's beauty and saying it must be a very special flower. The red daffodil heard what the crowd was saying. Now she was blushing with pride and held her head as high as all the other daffodils in the field.

The other daffodils were furious. "What a foolish crowd," said one indignantly. "We are the beautiful ones!" They turned their heads away from the red daffodil and ignored her. She began to feel unhappy again.

By now word had spread far and wide about the amazing red daffodil and people came from all over the land to see her. Soon, the king's daughter got to hear about the red daffodil. "I must see this for myself," said the princess. She set off with her servant and eventually they came to the field where the red daffodil grew. When the princess saw her, she clapped her hands with glee.

"The red daffodil is more beautiful than I ever imagined," she cried. Then she had an idea. "Please bring my pet dove," she said to her servant.

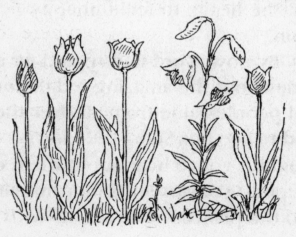

The man looked rather puzzled, but soon he returned with the bird. "As you know," said the princess to the servant, "I am to be married tomorrow and I would dearly love to have that red daffodil in my wedding bouquet."

The princess sent the dove into the middle of the field and it gently picked up the daffodil in its beak and brought her back to where the princess stood. The princess carried the daffodil back to the palace. She put the daffodil in a vase of water and there she stayed until the next day.

In the morning, the princess's servant took the red daffodil to the church. She could hear the bells and see all the guests assembling for the wedding ceremony. Then she saw the princess arrive in a coach driven by four white horses. How lovely the princess looked in her white gown and her head crowned with deep red roses.

As the servant reached the church door, the princess's lady-in-waiting stepped forward holding a huge bouquet of flowers into which she placed the red daffodil just as the flowers were handed to the princess. For a while, the red daffodil was overcome by the powerful scents of the other flowers in the bouquet, but when at last she looked

around her she realised, with astonishment, that all of them were red.
There were red daisies, red lilies, red
carnations and red foxgloves.
"Welcome," said one of the daisies,
"you're one of us." And for the first
time in her life, the red daffodil felt
really at home.

After the wedding, the princess scattered the flowers from her bouquet among the flowers in her garden. Every spring, when she opened her petals, the red daffodil found she was surrounded by lots of other red flowers, and she lived happily in the garden for many, many years.

The Sad Clown

BONGO THE CLOWN had a bit of a problem. Clowns were supposed to be happy, funny, jolly people, but Bongo was a very sad clown. Nothing at all seemed to make him laugh.

Whenever the circus came to town people from all around flocked to the big top hoping for an exciting day out. They thrilled to the daring performance of the high-wire act, as the acrobats leaped from one swinging trapeze to the next. They enjoyed the jugglers, who tossed bright, sparkling balls into the air while standing on one leg. And the crowd delighted in seeing the beautiful white horses parading

around the circus ring with the bareback riders balancing on their backs. When the seals came on, there was always a big cheer from the crowd, for everyone loved them and could watch their clever antics for hours.

But the biggest favourite of the crowd, especially with all the children, was the clown. Dressed in his big baggy trousers he would enter the circus ring with his funny walk. Everyone laughed to see him. They laughed even more when they saw his big floppy hat with the revolving flower on it. Even his painted clown face made them laugh.

But when his act started, the crowd thought they would burst with laughter. First of all his bicycle fell apart as he tried to ride around the ring. Then he fell out of his motor car when the seat tipped up.

By the time he had accidentally poured cold water down his trousers and fallen into the custard-filled swimming pool, the crowd were almost crying with laughter.

But beneath all the makeup, Bongo the sad clown wasn't smiling at all. In fact, he saw nothing funny at all in bicycles that fell apart as you used them, or cars that tipped you out as you went along, or having cold water poured down your

trousers, or even ending up face first
in a swimming pool full of custard.
He simply hadn't got a sense of
humour.

All the other performers in the
circus decided they would try and
cheer the sad clown up.

"I know," said the high-wire
trapeze acrobat, "let's paint an even
funnier face on him. That'll make
him laugh."

So that's what they did, but Bongo still didn't laugh and was still just as sad.

"Let us perform some of our tricks, just for him," said the seals.

So they sat on their stools and tossed their big coloured balls to each other, clapped their flippers together and made lots of honking sounds. But Bongo still didn't laugh. In fact, nothing that anyone tried made poor Bongo smile. He was still a very sad clown.

Then Percival the ring master spoke. "You know, I think I know what the problem is," he said. "There is nothing a clown likes better than playing tricks on other clowns.

Perhaps if we had a second clown, that would cheer Bongo up."

So right away they hired another clown, called Piffle.

The circus arrived in the next town and soon it was time for Bongo and Piffle's act. Piffle started riding around on his bike while Bongo pretended to wash the car by throwing a bucket of water over it. Instead of the water landing on the car, of course, it went all over Piffle, who just happened to be cycling past at that moment. A little smile flickered across Bongo's face at the sight of the soaking wet Piffle.

Next, Bongo and Piffle pretended to be cooking, and Bongo

tripped while carrying two huge custard pies. Both landed right in Piffle's face. Bongo let out a huge chuckle of laughter when he saw Piffle's custard-covered face.

At the end of their act, the clowns were pretending to be decorators, painting up a ladder. Of course, you've guessed it. The ladders fell down and all the pots of paint landed on the two clowns. Bongo looked across at Piffle, who had a big paint pot stuck on his head, with paint dripping down his body. Bongo threw back his head and roared with laughter. Piffle thought Bongo looked just as funny with paint all over his body, too. And as for the crowd — well, they thought two clowns were even funnier than one and they clapped and cheered and filled the big top with laughter. After that Bongo was never a sad clown again.

The Toys That Ran Away

P UT YOUR toys away, Lucy," said Lucy's mother from the kitchen, "it's time to get ready for bed." Lucy gave a great big sigh.

"Do I really have to?" she asked, knowing full well what the answer was going to be.

"Yes, of course you do," said her mother. "You shouldn't have to be told each time to put your toys away. You really don't look after them properly."

It was true. Lucy never had been very good at looking after her toys. Once she left her beautiful new doll outside in her pram and she had become ruined after it rained. Then she had carelessly dropped her tea set on the floor and some of the cups had broken. And she was forever just pushing all her toys back in the cupboard in a hurry, instead of putting them away carefully. Worse still, when she was in a temper, she would throw her toys, and sometimes she would even kick them.

Tonight Lucy was in another of her 'can't be bothered' moods. She grabbed a handful of toys and threw them into the cupboard. In first went some dolls, which all landed on their heads and then fell in a heap. Next Lucy threw in the little tables and chairs from the doll's house. They landed with a bounce and

came to a stop in the corner.
Without even looking behind her,
Lucy then picked up some puzzles
and a skipping rope, and tossed
them into the cupboard, too. They
landed with a crash on the floor of
the cupboard as well.

"That's that," said Lucy. She closed the cupboard door, squashing the toys even more, and went into the bathroom to have her bath.

Inside the toy cupboard Teddy, one of the toys, spoke. "I'm not going to stay here a moment longer," he said.

"Nor me," said Katie the ragdoll.

"If we aren't going to be loved, we aren't staying either," chimed the doll's house furniture.

"I want to be somewhere where I'm not thrown around," said one of the puzzles.

"So do we," said the roller blades.

One after another, all the toys

agreed that they weren't going to stay. They decided they would all go back to Toyland and wait to be given to some children who would love them more.

The next morning, Lucy decided that she would play with her skipping rope. When she opened the toy cupboard, she couldn't believe her eyes. All the toys had vanished. The shelves were completely empty.

At first Lucy thought her mother had moved them, but her mother said she hadn't.

"I expect you've put them somewhere yourself, Lucy, and can't remember where you've left them," said her mother, not very helpfully.

All day, Lucy searched high and low for her missing toys, but they were nowhere to be found. She went to bed in tears that night, wondering if she would ever be able to play with her toys again. She was already missing them terribly.

That night, Lucy was suddenly woken by a noise in her bedroom. Was she seeing things or was that a little fairy at the bottom of her bed? "Who are you?" asked Lucy.

"I am the special messenger from Toyland," replied the fairy. "I have been sent to tell you that all your toys have run away back to Toyland, because you treated them badly."

"Oh, I do miss my toys so much," cried Lucy.

"Well, if you really do, then you had better come and tell them yourself," said the fairy.

With that, the fairy floated over to Lucy and took her hand. The fairy then beat her wings so fast that they became a blur. At the same time Lucy felt herself being lifted from her bed. Out of Lucy's bedroom window they both flew, across fields and forests, until it became too misty for Lucy to see anything at all.

Suddenly, they were floating down to the ground. The mist lifted, and Lucy found herself in the grounds of a huge fairy-tale castle with tall, pointed turrets and warm, yellow lights twinkling from the windows.

"This is Toyland Castle," exclaimed the fairy, as she led Lucy to a large red door.

The fairy knocked on the door. "Do enter, please," said a voice.

Lucy found herself in a large, cosy room with a huge log fire.

Sitting in the corner was a kindly looking little man wearing a carpenter's apron and holding a broken wooden doll. "Hello," he said, "you've come to ask your toys to return, haven't you?"

"Well... er... yes," said Lucy, not really quite knowing what to say.

"It's up to them to decide, of course," said the little man. "They only come back here if they are mistreated. If they are broken, I repair them, and then they go to other children who love them more."

"But I do love my toys," wept Lucy.

"Then come and tell them yourself," smiled the little man.

He led Lucy into another room, and there, to her surprise, were all her toys. Not only that, but they were all shiny and new again. Nothing was broken or chipped or scratched. Lucy ran up to her toys.

"Please, toys, please come home again. I really do love you and miss you, and I promise I shall never mistreat you again," she cried. She picked up Teddy and gave him a big hug. Then she did the same thing to all the other toys.

"Well, it's up to the toys now," said the little man. "You must go back home again with the fairy messenger and hope that they will give you another chance."

With that, the fairy messenger
took Lucy's hand, and soon they
were floating over her own garden
again and through her bedroom
window. Lucy was so tired she didn't

even remember falling asleep when she got into bed.

In the morning she awoke, still rather sleepy, and rushed to the toy cupboard. There, neatly lined up on the shelves, were all her toys. Lucy was overjoyed. From that day on, she always treated her toys well and took great care of them.

Lucy never was quite sure whether the whole thing was a dream or not, but it certainly did the trick whatever it was.

There was one thing that really puzzled her though.

If it had just been a dream, why were all the toys so shiny and new again?